EQUATIONS

Praise for *Equations*

'In a city like Delhi, people of every class and creed work and live alongside one another, their lives overlapping but never truly meeting. Shivani Sibal delves into this complex intermingling through the stories of Rajesh and Aahan, whose lives are worlds apart and tightly intertwined. A story of class, power, and the shifting dynamics of modern India, *Equations* is an empathetic and multilayered novel.'

– Shashi Tharoor

'*Equations* tackles several contemporary and complex dynamics within multilayered Indian families with elan! It left me pretty breathless as I tried to keep up with the many surprising twists in the family saga, that tackles class and caste, politics and prejudice with sharp observations and terrific insights!'

– Shobhaa De

'Shivani Sibal's *Equations* portrays, with power and precision, worlds that exist next door to each other and are yet impossibly apart. Inhabited by men and women, parents and children, friends and lovers, each one fractured – and healed – by the irreversible forces of change. In her remarkably perceptive debut, Sibal shows how social mobility in today's India isn't just about aspiration, it's also shedding history to forge a future.'

– Raj Kamal Jha

'This riveting rags-to-riches story will fascinate readers as it spotlights the changing realities of the New India through powerful characters, exciting storytelling, suspenseful plot-twists and an insightful depiction of privilege and its costs. A great debut!'

– Chitra Banerjee Divakaruni

'Incisive and elegant, *Equations* holds up an unsparing mirror firmly to all the Indias we know – the India from our childhood to the India we live in, where ambition and privilege collide in the rarefied atmosphere of Lutyens' Delhi, resulting in an upheaval of all we held true about ourselves and those around us. A fabulous debut.'

– Kiran Manral

'A sparkling debut that ensconces the connubial trials of forgotten India.'

– Meghna Pant

EQUATIONS

SHIVANI SIBAL

HarperCollins *Publishers* India

First published in India by
HarperCollins *Publishers* 2021
A-75, Sector 57, Noida, Uttar Pradesh 201301, India
www.harpercollins.co.in

2 4 6 8 10 9 7 5 3 1

P-ISBN: 978-93-5422-757-8
E-ISBN: 978-93-5422-795-0

This is a work of fiction and all characters and incidents described in this book are the product of the author's imagination. Any resemblance to actual persons, living or dead, is entirely coincidental.

Typeset in 11/15.2 Minion Pro at
Manipal Technologies Limited, Manipal

Printed and bound at
Replika Press Pvt. Ltd.

MIX
Paper from
responsible sources
FSC www.fsc.org
FSC® C016779

This book is produced from independently certified FSC® paper
to ensure responsible forest management.

For Anina & Anisha

JUNE 2016

THE LAST OF the bags packed, Parul and Aahan Sikand were ready to leave their family home for the final time.

Acquired in 1946, Sikand House was intended to be the cradle for many grandsons and great-grandsons in the coming years. Displaced as he was at Partition, Rai Bahadur Manohar Krishna Sikand, Aahan's grandfather, a largely self-made man with a premonition about difficult times ahead, didn't suffer the life of a refugee, having swapped his house with that of an equally astute Muslim acquaintance before all the madness began. It was a gentleman's agreement.

The Rai Bahadur arrived in Delhi by air, with gold coins sewn into the lining of his and his wife's coats. Their worthy possessions had followed by road, including the heavy teak furniture and cast-iron cooking utensils that had been part of his wife's dowry.

As the family prospered in a new country still finding its feet, they hosted the leading industrialists of the time, and sheltered many a young, worse-off cousin, in Delhi to take an exam or for a job interview. Sikand House's lawns saw baithaks and performances, a young Farida Khanum had sung at Aahan's parents wedding, which Indira Gandhi herself had attended, at the height of both women's careers in the late 1960s.

There would be no place for this largesse in Aahan's future. A builder was to swiftly and efficiently raze Sikand House to the ground, and replace it with a block of carelessly constructed flats, where multiple families would take a piece of Rai Bahadur Sikand's dream, and plant their own in its place.

The June sun was unforgiving, with temperatures so high that even the mosquitoes couldn't survive. In better days, Aahan and Parul would have been holidaying in London around this time, drinking artisanal gin and tonics every evening at the South Audley pub with their friends from school, or parents of their children's friends – Delhiwalas with apartments in London.

Aahan walked out for the last time, abstractedly rearranging his thinning hair. Terrazzo would give way to Botticino, and the driveway where he had learnt to ride a bike was to be a stilt area in the new construction, where vacant-eyed servants would inhabit tiny, airless port-a-cabins, on the border of legality, inhaling the diesel-filled air that the generator would regularly spew into their rooms. The builder got permission from the municipal corporation to cut down the old Semal tree which his grandmother, his Dadi, had planted when she had moved there, the one in which hundreds of birds lived and sang at dawn and dusk. He vividly remembered playing with its cotton and pretending it was snow. Where it once stood would now be a parking spot, a precious and hotly contested piece of real estate in the new order of things. He would be returning here after it was rebuilt, to live in a flat, a three Bedroom-Hall-Kitchen unit, one bedroom for him and Parul, one for their children, and one for his mother, separated from his own with the thin, four-and-a-half-inch brick walls that the builders used now. The bedrooms in the new apartment were the size of the bathrooms in the old Sikand House, and no dressing rooms now of course. He would have to put the television on full blast to have sex with his wife.

Parul and him, used to occupying separate living quarters, like his parents before them, would now have to perform all the businesses of living – bathing, shaving, shitting, texting, toenail clipping – within a few feet of each other. Their children, a sulky teenaged girl and a prepubescent boy, would have to share a bedroom, and were aghast at the unfairness of it all. This was all that he could salvage from the mess that he was in, one amongst many flat owners, instead of the master of the house. He was lucky that he was even able to make the sale, shrouded as the property was with controversy. He got a raw deal, but it was better than no deal, and he was getting desperate.

Settling into the second-floor walk-up flat provided by the builder for his family to live in for the duration of the construction, Aahan tried to get used to apartment living for the first time in his life. He had grown up in the rambling Sikand compound, as its prince and heir. It had been like a warm blanket on a cold winter's night, and he hadn't ever summoned the will to get out of it – when the alarm rang, he hit snooze one time too many. Everything that he wanted had been placed exactly where he wanted it, not an inch to the left or the right, his entire life.

Their temporary home must have been a state-of-the-art affair when it was first constructed, twenty-odd years ago, when Delhi's smart set had begun to accept that they would have to get used to apartment living. The deficiencies in the builder-finish were now glaringly apparent. Most of the problems had to do with moisture-related damage; Indian construction folk through the ages had never managed to figure this one out. The faux-wooden flooring, so trendy when it first came out, had expanded, causing the dining room door to be permanently stuck, the fancy Italian-made taps had limescale stains like a map of the world, and the air conditioning leaked at designated spots across the house. It was the seepage in the living room that really got to him, though. In his opinion, seepage was a sign of poverty, of helplessness, of failure to improve one's lot. He had asked Parul, his once sweet Parul, to sort out some of these problems. He waited patiently, denied access to their bedroom while she chanted 'Nam Myoho Renge Kyo' for an hour and a half, and approached her whilst she was getting ready for lunch with their son's friends' moms, applying her makeup stooped over the shared bathroom sink – now that she no longer had a dressing table. She hadn't responded, and didn't remove her gaze from the mascara she was applying. She finished up, picked up a fire-engine red tweezer and decisively plucked a thick, black, stray hair from her chin, and looked up. 'Fuck off,' she said as she squeezed past him through the bathroom door into the bedroom.

What struck him about his current quarters was that the rooms just seemed so much closer together. Gone were the high ceilings, the multiple floors, the endless corridors, which in retrospect, had managed to keep the people in the house at a desirable distance. It seemed that his wife, mother and children were always in his way, not to mention the nameless, faceless and swiftly interchangeable servants, who dared to look him in the eye. There weren't any breakaway spaces for them either, the verandahs, terraces and laundry rooms where they went to smoke, flirt and gossip. The old retainers had left soon after they heard that the house was to be broken down, since the Sikands were no longer able to provide them with family accommodation.

Aahan dreamt of his Nani that night.

His beloved Nani, who had lived her last days in the tiny, dark, damp room allocated to her at the very top of Sikand House, from where her arthritic mobility was restricted, and her not having access to the rest of the house suited everyone. Nani's only son had married a Canadian woman and emigrated to Calgary, where he bought a house with the money his parents gave him. When his father was dead, leaving behind nothing, and the time came to look after her, he had offered to put her up in an old age home an hour's drive from his own place. Living with him wasn't an option, he had firmly said. There would be no Indian food there, and no one to talk to, with no desi television channels either. Even the ignominy of having a living son yet having to reside in her son-in-law's house was better than that. Inhabiting the smallest and most inaccessible room in the house befitted her reduced status of living in her daughter's sasural.

He dreamt of her paan daan, and of the plastic medicine beaker from which she drank shots of Old Monk neat – euphemistically referred to as 'mataji ki dawai' by the staff. No one really knew how the rum got up there. He was safe with her in that tiny room, lying in her single bed, in companionable silence, reading twin copies of *The Town Mouse and the Country Mouse* (someone had gifted him an extra copy) under the heavy, whirring fan, surrounded by pictures of Sai Baba, and of freedom fighters, Gandhi Ji and Jawaharlal Nehru, with his great-grandfather, Badi Nani's father, a big businessman at the time. These otherwise prized pictures couldn't grace other rooms of the house, it wasn't her house after all. Only the Sikands' pictures had that honour.

He had later discovered that she couldn't read English at all, that she had been humoring him all along.

The world couldn't reach him there, in his dream.

He woke up the next day, refreshed, and with more courage to face his fate than he did when he fell asleep. He tried his best to settle in. The Nespresso hadn't been unpacked; the kids were underfoot, their gadgets were everywhere, a tangle of PlayStation wires. Adding to the confusion, there was no water coming from any of the taps.

Later that morning, he got a call from the builder. 'One of the flats has already gone, from my share in the project,' he said. '*Rajesh Kumar ji ko hi diya hai*. MLA hai, he is even a minister now. It will be good for you, ghar ki security bani rahegi. Okay sir, jai mata di, sir.' He hung up.

The water supply resumed; all the taps belched and spewed a brownish liquid, and then suddenly water started flowing from everywhere, flooding everything.

Aahan Sikand and Rajesh Kumar. Son of Master and Servant.

PART ONE

ONE

New Delhi, the 1980s

'*Mr India mera favorite hai, Aahan bhaiya. Sridevi ka blue sari wala dance best hai!*' said Rajesh.

'*Haan, bari sahi lagti hai*,' replied an equally enthused Aahan.

They had seen it countless times, it was one of the few VCR tapes that Aahan possessed, along with a Woody Woodpecker cartoon and a World Wrestling Federation tape that someone had brought him as a gift from America. They didn't mind, they found companionship and comfort in its predictability, and Aahan often tackled his homework while watching the tapes.

Aahan and Rajesh sat in the drawing room upstairs, the one with the round dining table and the dusty green chandelier, waiting for the eight o'clock movie to start on Doordarshan. Even the advertisements were a joy to watch – the pretty girl dancing under the waterfall was a favorite.

Aahan, the only son, born after two sisters – much to the relief of his parents – got pride of place in front of the brown window air conditioner. His playmate, Rajesh, was the son of his father's servant. Rajesh left his blue-and-white Bata rubber chappals outside the room whenever he entered, as he had been instructed to do, and settled himself down on the floor just beside where Aahan was sprawled on the sofa – with Choopey, the family dog, next to him – his feet resting on the coffee table. Neither of the boys ever questioned this arrangement. This was just how it had been, since they were born, Rajesh a year younger, with his nut-brown complexion and misshapen teeth, who wasn't allowed to touch anything when he was in the kothi watching television on Sunday, or whenever Aahan felt like having him around.

The electricity went, and Rajesh shut his eyes in the dark by reflex. 'Oh-ho,' said Aahan, exasperated. There was no way of knowing when it would come back, could be minutes, or hours, or indeed the entire night could pass without respite or information. His mother entered the room with a torch, and Rajesh automatically stood up. Laxman, Rajesh's father, followed her. She patted Rajesh on the head, and waved him down. He took his place on the floor again.

Laxman Kumar had worked there since he was a boy, ten or eleven, he wasn't quite sure of his age.

He remembered his village clearly. His mother bent over the wood fire, making chapatis; shuffling along to school with his canvas satchel; learning multiplication tables by rote; the school headmaster's grey walking stick; his father tending to the fields with his uncles.

Laxman's parents died when he was just a boy, in a train collision. Their bodies had been found clinging to one another's, taken by surprise. He was alone, a liability. His uncles decided to send him to work in Delhi, one less claimant to the land, one less mouth to feed.

Laxman's Chhoti Ma, his Chachi, organized for her cousin from a neighboring village to bring him to Sikand House, as his own assistant, unbeknownst to his masters. Laxman was to live outside his quarter, a sixty-square-foot room with damp blue walls, his clothes on hooks, a calendar that the sahib had given him, and a plastic mirror.

There was a sheltered landing outside this room where he was allowed to sleep, and he was comfortable there. He slept on a cot and kept his clothes and things below, folded in a plastic bag from a shoe shop in South Extension, he wasn't sure how he had come to possess it. A part of the meal served to his benefactor was saved and given to Laxman to eat on an old newspaper, and the occasional coin to spend in the market while on an errand.

Laxman was only a child with no skills. In return for washing his clothes, cleaning his room, and running odd jobs for him, he did not receive a salary, just the privilege of room and board, of safety from the world. In time, he was noticed by the Rai Bahadur, Aahan's grandfather, who turned a blind eye to the arrangement, occasionally patting the boy on his head and giving him a toffee from the stash he kept for his children. Aahan's Dadi protested, but was overruled by her husband.

Soon, Laxman's Chachi's cousin, his protector, was caught stealing ghee. He would put it on bread and eat it if he got hungry at night, when the kitchen was locked. He was immediately dismissed. The bari memsahib ran a tight ship, and she had an exacting inventory of every drop, grain and morsel procured in her head, and the idea that someone had gotten the better of her was too much to tolerate.

The Rai Bahadur decreed that the boy could stay on, unpaid.

It was from there that he rose, becoming the man for all seasons: driver, handyman, cook, gardener, gopher. These ubiquitous talents, along with the fact that he knew no other life, earned him the tag of 'loyal' and he was eventually allowed to bring his wife along with him to share the tiny quarter outside which he had once slept, with the cooking range outside, and the shared bathroom for all the staff downstairs – with exposed cement, a single tap, and an Indian-style loo. He had brought his bride, a maid working in the neighborhood, there.

His only son, Rajesh, was born a few years later, in a missionary hospital nearby, late into the evening, to which his wife had gone in a rickshaw because the family car might have gotten soiled. It was a rainy night, but it couldn't be helped. Aahan's mother was mildly annoyed because she had a dinner party to attend, and had to cancel her plans, stay back and look after her son.

Aahan, her son, had been under Babita, Rajesh's mother's care since he was born.

Babita had worked in a house nearby as an ayah and married Laxman at a temple nearby. Their romance had blossomed while they were out walking their employers dogs, a ferocious Doberman for Babita and a gaggle of Pekingese for the Sikand family. An unusual arrangement, but neither had any relatives who cared enough to stop them. Babita, born Barbara, was a Christian girl who grew up in an orphanage in Jharkhand, where her mother had left her. When she came to Delhi to work, none of the other domestic help could pronounce her name, and so it was changed by consensus to Babita for convenience.

As a nod to his growing status, Laxman was allowed to decorate his quarter with flowers to welcome his bride. She was permitted to live there with her husband, and was to become the Rai Bahadur's daughter-in-law's personal maid.

She worked quickly and cheerfully, and when Aahan was born, it was decided that she would be his nanny.

The Rai Bahadur had died before Aahan came, never having seen his grandson. His heart just stopped one day, without warning. He went in his sleep, unexpectedly, like the blessed do. His wife had a stroke in shock, and was confined to her room in her last years, a vegetable. Aahan's parents were in charge now.

Aahan had been quickly weaned from his mother, and she resumed her normal life of cocktail parties and late mornings and salon visits and lunches. The infant was given a room on another floor of the house, so that the noise he made over the years – crying, screaming, laughing, growing – wouldn't disturb his mother. He was watched and fed and bathed and changed by Babita, with just a break of forty days when she gave birth to Rajesh, when Aahan was just a year old. There had been pressure to return quickly, else someone new would have to be found 'temporarily'. Babita knew what this meant, and asked for permission to take her own son with her to the nursery, her workplace. This was quickly granted. Aahan's sisters were already in school, and his mother was used to being the master of her own time. The care of an infant frayed her nerves and she was ready to hand over the child as soon as possible, but to someone responsible – he was her only son, after all.

Spending less time with his mother and more with Babita and Rajesh, he took to calling her 'ma', a word that she had kept repeating to her own infant son. Initially, the year's age gap between them seemed vast. While her son was too small to speak, Aahan was primed to learn, to imitate, and no amount of correction could stop him from doing so. He started calling his mother 'Mummy' and Babita 'Ma'.

Babita enjoyed this control that she had over the young prince, even actively encouraged it. She couldn't help but break into a satisfied grin when the young, crying scion had to be pried loose from her arms to go to his mother if there was a visitor. 'Naughty-naughty mat karo, mummy ke paas jao', she would say in an infuriating tone that drove Aahan's mother crazy, but she took a few deep breaths and kept calm; good help was so difficult to find these days. Another significant perk of the position was that most of Aahan's old clothes – not just the ones stained with bananas or oil or some other impossible-to-remove food item or worse – came to Rajesh. Memsahib couldn't be bothered with sorting the old clothes, she had no intention of having another child, and so they were useless to her. The task fell on Babita, who relished it, devising a three-tier system – the best ones, in mint condition, for Rajesh, followed by the acceptable, which could be cleaned and mended, for the other servants who were in her good books, followed by the damaged ones for the part-time workers, the cleaners and the gardeners, who couldn't hope for better. Those she disapproved of were left out completely. Babita loved dressing up her son, especially when they went out.

As Aahan grew into a large, active toddler, inquisitive, bored and noisy, his mother organized for Laxman to take them on outings. Babita was to mind him, with Rajesh taken along as a companion. Babita sat in the front, with the two children rolling about unselfconsciously in the back. It was during these visits, for ice cream at India Gate, to the zoo where they threw stones at the monkeys, and once to Appu Ghar, that Babita pretended to herself, just for a little while, that she was the Memsahib, out with her husband and well-dressed children on an excursion, which made her life as a servant more bearable.

There was a birthday party – Aahan's cousin was turning three. The child's parents owned a number of petrol stations, were connected, and had the most lavish parties for their children, with elephant rides, free flowing soft drinks, and imported return presents. 'I can't manage him alone,' Aahan's mother said to her husband, who was getting ready for work, changing his shirt multiple times, sucking his gut in while looking in the mirror. 'I won't be able to take Aahan to the party without Babita to look after him, he is just too active and I want to chat with people. Plus the girls will be there too. But does that mean that I have to let her bring her son?' She didn't get a response; he was still preoccupied with his appearance. 'I'll take Babita, and her boy too,' she said to no one in particular.

On the day of the event, Babita readied Aahan while Madam got dressed, and then ran up to the quarter to get Rajesh presentable. '*Chalo, chalo, jaldi karo, joote pehno!*' she urged. His wet hair was parted on the left side and he wore Aahan's birthday party outfit from the year before: a pair of brown-and-white shorts, T-shirt and suspenders number, with talcum powder liberally dusted on his neck. They met Madam and Aahan at the gate. '*Chalo, aage baitho, Rajesh ko apne saath rakho*,' said Memsahib. They set off across Delhi, with Laxman driving the Contessa Classic, Babita in front with Rajesh on her lap. Luckily, her sari was synthetic and wouldn't get creased. Aahan, his mother and sisters occupied the rear seat.

On arrival, Laxman opened the door for Madam and her children, and Babita and Rajesh followed a few steps behind, carrying Aahan's water bottle from home. The gift was given to the birthday child, and Aahan's mother wandered off to socialize with her acquaintances, leaving Babita in charge of the boys. There were a number of games organized, and they didn't manage to pin the tail on the donkey. Aahan won a small plastic faux-video game in hoopla, which he gave to Rajesh because it was pink.

It was time for musical chairs, and ten-or-so children crowded around the moodas. It was September, oppressive and humid. They jogged round the low cane stools in time to the music, which the birthday child's Mami would periodically switch off. One by one, all the kids were eliminated, except for Rajesh, Aahan, and Hammad, a Yemeni boy who lived next door; his parents worked at the embassy.

The competition was intense. The music went on forever, and Aahan zoned out. It was 'Born in the USA', one of his favourite songs. The music stopped, Hammad took one seat, and Aahan was in front of the other. Before he realized it, Rajesh had lunged forward, pushing him ever so slightly, not enough for it to be noticed by the judges and have him disqualified, and taken the seat.

Aahan was out of the game, and Rajesh was in. Babita wiped Aahan's hot, angry tears as Rajesh continued in the competition, focused, unaware. Hammad won, and Rajesh walked up to his mother dejected, only to be greeted by a stinging slap. Rajesh absorbed his subservience to Aahan at a cellular level, his mother had communicated the benefits of this behavior to him like a lesser animal might teach its young how to hunt or forage. He had known from an early age that his mother would put him down and pick up Aahan if he wanted; that he would always get to pick which toy to play with second.

As long as the rules were in place, calm and camaraderie remained between the boys. Rajesh even learnt how to put up just enough of a fight in their games for it to seem competitive, and to lose at the right time. These lessons didn't come easy. When Aahan won, he would slap Rajesh on the back and offer him imported chocolates that his mother kept locked in a fridge in her dressing room. When Rajesh won, sometimes it happened by sheer probability, it was followed by a long sulk, silence, and often with him being sent to the quarter, with his mother staying behind with her charge. He began to value success over victory, letting glory go to get what he actually wanted.

Rajesh felt lucky to be born in the kothi. His uncle – they weren't related really, but he was from the orphanage his mother had grown up in back in Jharkhand – lived in Jagdambika Camp, a slum near the railway tracks. Rajesh and his parents visited them sometimes, but couldn't invite them over to visit at Sikand House. Aahan's parents didn't allow the servants to have visitors in the compound, even in the quarter. Madam Aunty, as Rajesh called Aahan's mother, didn't want strange people walking around the house under any circumstances, even if there were emergencies in the staff's families. His friends at Jagdambika heard about the house and its lavish riches – indoor plumbing, the refrigerator, and how air conditioning felt on your skin – through the tales that Rajesh told them, painting a mythical paradise, Elysium. It was rivaled in status only by the boy whose family lived in independent quarters at the crematorium, who could have visitors, where you could go and see bodies burning while playing with kites on the open terrace.

The camp was near the industrial area where Sahib Uncle's factory was, and several people who lived there worked for him. It was relatively better than the other settlements that lined the railway land all across the city. Jagdambika faced the tracks, and the passing trains were the soundtrack to the residents' lives. The streets dividing the shanties were not too narrow, and there was rudimentary lighting at night, bringing crime down, and a better ratio of shared toilets, stinky and semi-functional as they were, to people. The best huts were those that faced the railway line, where air and light and movement were possible. Some of the interiors of the worst slums were still and dark and hopeless, and where one lived in the scheme of things had a direct bearing on the occupants' constitution and disposition. Indeed, the people who lived along the railway line seemed more cheerful and positive. Whether it was because of the space to sit out and watch the trains go by, or the energy of the people on the trains itself, no one could say for sure. But certainly, those who lived in the airless boxes at the heart of the slum were comparatively melancholic and unfriendly, and always ready for a fight.

The slum dwellers lived an enforced collective life, which Rajesh enjoyed watching though he wouldn't want to live there. He nevertheless liked to dip into the huts of his parents' friends. The women who were employed outside the home cooked and cleaned in houses nearby, and the men mostly worked in the factories in the adjoining industrial area. This was the primary reason why people wouldn't relocate to the resettlement colonies, which the government was offering – they were a one-hour bus ride away, with not even a Mother Dairy booth nearby. There was the neighbor whose enterprising son had started breeding Great Danes, keeping the two beasts that he had stolen from a kothi whose owners were usually abroad, tied up outside their hut along the railway line. The dogs barked madly every time the trains passed, but were overall docile around humans. There was the northeastern girl, a beautician who had married a handsome bouncer, and her children with soft black hair, wheatish skin, and almond-shaped eyes. She ran a beauty salon in the slum called Face and Figure. Waxing, threading, hair styling, nail polishing, massage, party makeup – they provided every service except washing hair of course, as there was no running water. Babita often commented that the women from the slum looked much younger and prettier than the ladies who came for kitty parties at the kothi, and put this down to their constant physical activity and fresh diet, a byproduct of the absence of refrigeration. She felt strongly about this and mentioned it often.

As they started school, Aahan was enrolled at the best private institution in the city, and Rajesh at the local Sarvodaya Vidyalaya, fixed up through a contact of Sahib's. They began to grow apart, amicably and organically. School for Aahan was when competition first began. Who brought imported snacks in their tiffin boxes? Who had the fanciest watch, who had the latest magnetic pencil box, who went where for a vacation, who had the bigger car, the more famous relatives? It all began then, and never left his psyche. For

Rajesh, pretty much all the kids at his school had the same things, or nothing. Vacations were in the village, either with maternal or paternal grandparents, or, in the case of Rajesh, nowhere. Everyone brought greasy parathas and a sabzi to school, the same that their fathers took to their workplaces, employed as factory workers and drivers and, lower down in the hierarchy, security guards. They all came to school in a rickshaw, or walking beside their mothers, or riding pillion on their fathers' scooters or bicycles. The unfortunate ones were the ones whose fathers beat them or their mothers, or worse, the children of widows and abandoned women, living in a corner of their maternal homes, the ones who suddenly lost their jobs and quarters, the girls who were sexually assaulted but kept quiet, and those who silently went through their school lives without learning, understanding nothing that was taught and had nobody who cared.

Relative to the lives that he saw around him, Rajesh viewed himself as privileged. His family lived together in a neighbourhood surrounded by parks and playgrounds, he could ride the cycle which Aahan no longer wanted and he wore clothes which his peers couldn't afford, Aahan's clothes. The Sahib and Memsahib were kind and relatively predictable in their behaviour, as were his parents. He spent a lot of his spare time with the maali, helping him water the lawn, learning about the soil and plants and seasons, watering the lawn and getting wet, and accepting Babita's inevitable scolding cheerfully. He began to grow some hardy plants in his own space, the balcony outside his parents' quarter, the same spot that his father had occupied when he arrived as a child at Sikand House. He planted simple stuff to begin with, syngonium and money plants, graduating to successfully maintaining a bougainvillea creeper which erupted in a defiant, cheerful fuchsia, offset against the rest of the dull, grey quarter block.

Rajesh was taken along to places that he wouldn't have normally accessed, and his spoken English was better than all his classmates thanks to Aahan. He ate well and generally met with kindness.

Gradually, as the years passed, and they grew up, Aahan and Rajesh became more conscious of their respective places in the Sikand House hierarchy. People stopped treating Rajesh as a child, more like a young half-servant. The kindness and largesse shown to him as a boy wore off as he grew, and the people around him stopped seeing him as cute – his fuzzy upper lip and cracking voice didn't help. The last time that he went on an outing, as a companion, with Aahan was to the Delhi Gymkhana Club annual Christmas party, when they were around ten years old, and he and his mother weren't allowed to attend, and were asked to wait in the ladies' bathroom with the other ayahs while Aahan and his mother were at the party. Nothing personal, club rules. No servants were allowed in the main club areas, and in the eyes of the management he too was one, therefore not permitted to be introduced as a guest.

When they were around five and six years old, Rajesh performed the aarti during Laxmi puja at Diwali alongside Aahan. Their own lack of awareness about their stations meant that they were inseparable then and it seemed only normal. No one knew exactly when Rajesh lost his place as amongst the first to do the Laxmi puja; it had never been his anyway. He hadn't been instructed to do so, but over the years, Rajesh naturally retreated to his appropriate spot at the rear of the gathering, behind the family and senior servants.

TWO

WAITING OUTSIDE THE lawyer's office for interminable hours was difficult for Aahan. He was born with a place in this world, as the scion of the Sikand family, and took having to wait anywhere, or indeed any delay or inconvenience, however minor or justified objectively, as a personal affront, a marker of his diminished status. If that wasn't bad enough, Parul insisted on accompanying him to every meeting and hearing. After all, it was through her uncle's connections that the lawyer was giving them his time, this reduced fee, the commitment that he would actually show up when the case was listed. This gave her a sense of entitlement to comment nonstop about what should be done, could have been done, and wasn't being done. The factory was in a mess, there were labour problems, and there was the whole larger Nooriya problem to tackle. The lawyer who he was consulting was a school acquaintance too – one who he wouldn't have deigned to acknowledge in the school yard, possibly even bullied, and certainly never invited to his parties – and Parul's Mausaji's intervention was needed to ensure that he met them quickly. And now, here he was, hoping that the learned senior counsel gave him adequate attention and would reach the court in time for the hearing, give it priority over his other cases. The bills were astronomical whether the lawyers got the job done or not. Plus, he had to keep up appearances in his personal life too: business-class travel, imported cars, a lavish annual bash. The factory was mortgaged, the Shimla house title was unclear. He wouldn't get much for it, even if it did come to him.

Someone more important than him entered the office, with a flurry of activity. ADCs, security people, hangers-on followed. Mr More Important was ushered straight into Aahan's classmate's room, and his wait got a lot longer. He sighed and resigned himself to staring vacantly at the ticker on the screen before him, where a news channel was streaming on mute: 'BREAKING NEWS: RESHUFFLE IN DELHI CABINET'.

Completely disinterested in politics, Aahan was about to tune off, when he saw a name chug by on the rolling list of ministerial berths: Rajesh Kumar, minister for Labour and Social Welfare.

How had he done it, making it look so effortless, seemingly overnight? Aahan smiled, despite himself, at the grit and gumption of his one-time playmate. He remembered his father, smirking when he heard that Rajesh had joined this new crackpot party, that he spent his time in Jagdambika

Camp, supervising water tankers sent by the party to be delivered to those wretched people – they didn't have a water connection, of course – even carrying the heavy buckets without spilling the precious liquid to the older ladies' homes. His father had patronizingly instructed Laxman Chacha to make Rajesh leave all this nonsense, he would get him a government peon's job through his connections, which was the best that he could hope for, after all. *Kya chaihiye usko zindagi se, Laxman?* He would ask, while idling at a traffic light. Laxman would smile and nod deferentially, and keep his eyes on the road.

Despite all the pressure and advice to the contrary, when it seemed like madness, Rajesh had forged on, and here he was, a minister in the state government. Aahan made a mental note to ask Rajesh if he could help him resolve the disputes with the factory labour union, to get them off his case and let him close down the unit without too much trouble. He glanced at Parul, but by the looks of it, she had seen the news too. Her face pursed in a grim frown, exposing the cracks in her makeup, where it had settled into the inevitable crevices and creases on her once youthful profile. The harsh bluish office lighting gave her face an orangey hue and highlighted the crow's feet along her eyes. He knew his wife only too well, she wasn't happy with this development, and was calculating how this would affect them, how it could potentially be used to their benefit.

They would remember 2015 as the year when Rajesh, their servant's son, was a minister in the government, and they were looking to sell everything to stay afloat. Parul was thinking back to the day when she thought, in retrospect, that it all began to go downhill. It would have been 18 April, Aahan's birthday, about a decade ago, give or take a year or two.

It had been an unusually hot April, hot enough for her to remember it a decade later. Haryana had temporarily stopped supplying water to Delhi, and there was none in the house. People like her didn't know anyone who mattered in the local government any more. It was full of the riffraff jhuggi-jhopri types now, she felt – uneducated louts who had previously hung around akharas, teashops and brothels. Most of her father's classmates had secured government jobs when they left college, IAS and IRS officers, or in the army like her Papa, with one old boy even becoming a minister in Uttarakhand. If they ever needed anything done, there had always been someone that Papa or Mausaji could call. No one from Parul's and Aahan's class had even given the joint services exam, it just wasn't considered an attractive option. As a result, now that Papa and his batchmates had retired, they had no one to call for conveniences like water, electricity, school admissions, street sweeping, drain cleaning.

Parul and Aahan had a large party planned that night, for Aahan's birthday. That it was a weeknight didn't bother any of the guests. The men mostly worked in businesses established by their fathers, with no specific hours of work, and the women didn't work at all. Rajesh would be the bartender, of course. He could be trusted not to steal the booze. He didn't drink, and he wouldn't dare take a bottle to sell. In those days, he still occasionally stayed in the servant quarter block with his parents, sleeping outside their room on a rolled-up mattress that was stowed under their bed when it wasn't in use. Rajesh had offered to organize a water tanker for them; the councilor was his 'friend', he said. Aahan had accepted while slapping Rajesh on the back: '*Dost, tere to kaafi contacts ban gaye, nayi sarkaar mein, ab mera saara kaam tu hi karaana.*'

And yes, that was how it was going to be.

For the occasion, Parul decided to wear her blue lace LK Bennett dress, the one that didn't really work without Spanx – if she was to be honest with herself, was still a bit meaty even with it – and the three-carat diamond solitaire earrings that she had borrowed from her Masi for the evening. She wondered what it would take to get her own pair. She descended the staircase, carefully, her nude heels were a bit ambitious and she hoped that no one would notice that they were slightly scuffed, to find that Aahan had already started on the whiskey.

She sighed. She had loved drinking when she was in college and still did, really, but having to keep an eye on Aahan every single time he consumed alcohol, which was every day, substantially dampened the fun. How many had it been? How quickly? Had he eaten? Would he stagger home cheerfully, or would he be in a mood to fight? Would the kids notice? A minder now, she was always in control, approaching drunkenness as she would a reunion with her school girlfriends – extremely enjoyable for the evening, always without her husband, and at best an occasional event.

Parul had met Aahan at The Tipsy, an all-white themed bar that kids from Modern School and Vasant Valley frequented. They had spotted each other there every Saturday for a couple of months. Both had been partying with their own, separate set of friends. An army child, she had studied at an all-girls boarding school in the mountains since she was little, while her parents lived in the mofussil cantonment towns where her father was posted, Bareilly and Jalandhar and Ajmer. When it was time for university, she had to study in Delhi. Her parents' budget did not allow for the shiny foreign universities that were in all the bulky catalogues that arrived in the mail and SAT classes and her friends' incessant chatter in the school canteen those last months of term, before everyone went their own way. Most of her classmates were to study abroad, and her three best friends had gotten admission in the same mid-western US college. 'Parul, yaar, you have to come! Only two of us can be roommates so one of us will be left out! Tell your dad to work something out na, it will be such fun!' they trilled. Life was just beginning.

She joined a private university near Delhi, more competitive than an Ivy League in its acceptance rate, but that was because there were just so many applicants for everything in India. She lived on campus during the week and spent the weekend at her Masi's house – the one who lived in Delhi – in her cousins' empty rooms, with their photographs and stuffed toys from childhood for company. Those cousins were working abroad now.

Her Masi was married to a prominent celebrity doctor in the city, who was not averse to sheltering well-connected patients in his clinic to evade jail time, producing medical certificates at a price, and admitting them into his clinic should a brush with the law arise. The clinic rooms were exorbitantly priced, at par with a hotel, to compensate for the extra service, and had all the comforts of a five-star hotel available for patients, at an additional cost, off menu. Masi's family lived a lifestyle that Parul hadn't previously enjoyed, either at school, which institutionalized discomfort for its own sake, or at the small towns where her parents lived. Their house was a design triumph, all glass and steel, overlooking a pristine park and medieval monument in the front, and the rear of other people's homes with their laundry and water tanks and iron grills at the back. It was once featured in a lifestyle magazine, with pictures of Mausaji, Masi and her cousins. She had watched the photoshoot from the sidelines.

College life had come to an end, and she had stretched it to the maximum with an MA. She now had a job with a publishing house that specialized in coffee-table books. It didn't pay much, but then, they didn't expect much in return either, leaving her free on evenings and weekends to socialize, exercise and take forward Project Husband. Her fifteen-thousand-rupee salary wasn't going to get her where she needed to be for decades, or ever. She was at the mercy of an ill-humoured older lady boss, a chain-smoker who made the entire office reek, but it was overall worth it.

All through college, she had dated just one boy, older than her. A beautiful soul, she had thought. Kamal-Jensyn Mitra was an artist, the son of a prominent Bengali adman and a Swedish mother. She had given herself to the relationship completely and quickly, the bohemian environment of his home in Lutyens' Delhi ensuring that she could stay nights with him at his room in the annexe there, and breakfast with his parents the next morning. It was most irregular, but her parents didn't know, or pretended not to know, and Masi seemed to believe she was staying on campus. She had high hopes of the relationship, which came crashing down when she arrived unexpectedly there one day to find him in bed with the woman who used to come regularly to give massages to the entire family on the professional massage table that they had imported from Thailand. In fact, she had once even given Parul a back massage when she had stayed over.

He wasn't too perturbed to see her, though his partner scurried away, quickly putting on faded panties and a too-small bra, which looked like hand-me-downs, and a kurti with jeans. She slipped into flip-flops, her chipped silver nail polish insolently on display. He was an artist, he explained, and sex was part of the constant rediscovery of his senses. She raged, fumed and broke a crystal ashtray while he smoked a cigarette and watched, stubbing out the remains in the empty carton. Parul went to his mother to try and make him see sense, but she was foreign, and didn't understand the Indian ways. No one had compelled her to sleep with him, her almost-mother-in-law had helpfully pointed out.

Completely distraught, she went home, to her real home, where her parents were, in Kanpur, to lick her wounds. They were worried about her, but the years spent apart meant that they just didn't know how to communicate with her. Her father talked about the weather and the regimental party uncomfortably at the breakfast table where she sat glassy eyed. Her mother suggested marriage alliances with young army officers. How could Parul explain to her mother that she would rather die than live the life that she had led, attending regimental dances and organizing donation drives for martyred jawaans' families? She begged them to send her abroad to study, just for a year, to move on. They just couldn't afford it, and that was the end of it.

Her leave period ended and she returned to Delhi, to the news that her best work-friend was getting married to the scion of a wealthy Dubai family. As she attended her friend's wedding, she vowed that she wasn't going to get it wrong the next time round.

The divide that the equalizing atmosphere of boarding school and her natural good looks had so far bridged would now grow. Her looks would inevitably fade. Her friends would now have expensive educations and weddings and jewelry and addresses that her parents could not afford to buy for her. In the real world, it did not matter that she had once been house captain at school or that she topped in English literature in her class. It mattered that her peers were getting BMWs for their twenty-first birthdays, while she was paying EMIs on her Santro with her own salary. Soon, her father would retire and her parents would move to their flat in Dwarka, and she wouldn't be able to justify living at Masi's anymore. And then she would be an army-background girl living in Dwarka with her retired parents, driving her Santro-on-EMIs to work. She remembered the lines that she had read in *The Prime of Miss Jean Brodie*:

> 'One's prime is elusive. You little girls, when you grow up, must be on the alert to recognise your prime at

whatever time of your life it may occur. You must then live it to the full.'

She had to move quickly for the transfer to be seamless.

It was she who approached Aahan first, asking him if he had a cigarette though she did not smoke, something that her instant coughing fit made apparent to him. He burst into laughter and offered her a drink, suggesting an elaborate cocktail, but she wanted a glass of champagne. He ordered her a demi, and when she saw the half-sized bottle arrive, she said, 'Oh, this is called an addha, in this country.' He chuckled again. He liked this girl. They got talking, and he told her about his sisters, the factory, how he loved smoking up, about his house – she gathered that it was a kothi. She wasn't used to the champagne, it went to her head quickly. A little drunk, Parul leaned over and kissed him gently, not intending to offer more. 'It must be the bubbly. Thanks!' she said, and left, without giving him her phone number. He hadn't asked.

About a week later, she got a call from Aahan, who had impressively managed to get her number, asking her to watch the World Cup final at his house with his friends and him. She refused, saying that she was busy that evening. Another invite followed soon after, to have dinner with him – alone. At his place.

He lived alone in a tiny room on the top of the house, no one would disturb them there. She refused. Undeterred, he called again, telling her that he had booked a table at Tatsuya, the hottest Japanese restaurant in town, and told her she couldn't refuse as it had been really difficult to organize. She accepted. Wearing a fitted, but not-too-tight dress, impossibly high heels and carrying her Masi's Chanel bag, she met him at the porch of her aunt's house and noted that he picked her up in a Mercedes. Some of her former classmates from college were at the restaurant too, there was a birthday of someone in another group. She greeted them and introduced Aahan. Many of them knew him anyway, and the couple then settled down at their own table. He ordered a bottle of Moët & Chandon. She was going to stay in the club where she wanted to belong, but as a permanent member this time.

Against conventional wisdom, she slept with him pretty quickly. He found this disarming, a change from the usual chase-around, something so simple and natural. She started coming over regularly to Sikand House, but their encounters usually took place at Masi's, where she had started living after college ended. Masi was aware of these visits but turned a blind eye. The girl had to be settled, time was running out.

When she went over to his house, she sat in the living room with his mother, and never asked to see his bedroom. His sisters were divided in their opinion of her, ranging from 'sweet girl' to 'climber'. She chatted with his mother's friends, and updated the sisters on the latest gossip about their school friends – many of their younger siblings were in her age group and larger social network. She brought small but thoughtful gifts – a flattering shade of nail polish, diet snacks, mithai from Kanpur where her father was now posted. Within a year of their first drink together, he proposed, taking her to Agra for the day (she insisted she wouldn't travel with him overnight while they were boyfriend and girlfriend). Parul had been briefed by Masi on how to handle the situation. Against her instinct, she didn't accept immediately. She smiled and told him that she loved him, looked at the two-carat diamond, a bit smaller than she had imagined, and told him that she would have to think about it. Aahan insisted that she put on the rock anyway. She complied, and since they ironically couldn't even exchange a light kiss at the Taj Mahal, she hugged him instead. He told her that there was another surprise waiting. He had booked a room at the Amarvilas hotel, where there was a bottle of pink champagne chilling. There, he fucked her gently and attentively, and she couldn't hold out any longer. She accepted his proposal, and they were engaged. They returned to Delhi where she first went to take Aahan's mother's blessings.

A small, formal engagement ceremony was held soon after, at Masi's house, and Parul pulled out all the stops, within her parents' limited budget. There were flowers everywhere, just one kind – desi gulab, procured from the mandi where they were sold much cheaper – hanging in ladis from the doorways and decapitated and captured in glass bowls, their fragrance enveloping the house in an almost overwhelming cloud. Mithai was served in Masi's silver platters, and Parul wore her cousin's Anamika Khanna lehenga from her best friend's wedding, no one was the wiser for it. She was even allowed to take it in a bit since it was from her cousin's pre-Atkins days. She paid the makeup artist with her own money, half a month's pay.

The rituals were to be in the late morning. After the puja, they exchanged rings, the same princess-cut diamond solitaire for Parul and a simple gold band, with the date that they first met engraved inside, for Aahan. The entire alcohol budget was allocated to six bottles of Veuve Clicquot, served in champagne coupes – Mausaji thought they were superior to flutes – with artisanal chocolates, also courtesy her cousin, who had brought them back from Selfridges.

'Everything has gone off beautifully,' Masi declared, after the ladkawalas left.

That evening, Parul and Aahan were to attend a sangeet, of Parul's school friend. He returned to pick her up in the evening – in the new Porsche Cayenne gifted to him by his father for his engagement – coming inside to greet his new in-laws. He had a whiskey with Mausaji and Daddy, and they were ready to go. Parul was still wearing the same lehenga, but had removed the maang tikka and let down her waist-length hair from the morning's prim updo into bold waves to make it more appropriate for another person's event.

'I'm still wearing the makeup from the morning, looks good na?' She asked Aahan as they drove into the farm, a Spanish hacienda in Chattarpur – mining money from Madhya Pradesh.

He looked at her, smiled, got out of the driver's seat and opened the passenger side door for her. The event was a qawwali, and Parul felt appropriately dressed up. She always had a moment of hesitation when she entered a party that she had gotten it all wrong. They went to greet the couple, who were perforce sitting on the floor, at the front row of the mehfil. They had no interest in the music, the mining baron father of the girl fancied himself as a patron of the arts and thought that it would be a high-class thing to do. Parul had occupied the desk behind the bride, Parisa, through most of their school years, where seating was alphabetical. She sat down beside her friend to keep her company. She quite enjoyed qawwali, and knew the 101 ones, '*Yeh jo halka halka*' and '*Piya ghar aaya*' – garden variety stuff. Aahan rolled his eyes and wandered off to the bar. Parisa was clutching Parul's hand, she couldn't follow him. The music was deafening up front, and Parul moved a bit to the side, still towards the front.

She spotted out of the corner of her eye, Kamal Jensyn, her first boyfriend, and her heart skipped a beat. He came and joined her, sitting down close to her left – it was crowded. She looked at him and couldn't help but break into a wide grin. He felt the ring on her finger and said something inaudible; the music was too loud. Just then, Aahan returned, a couple of shots down. He was looking for his fiancée.

Aahan saw her sitting with Kamal Jensyn and went black with anger. He walked right past the length of the qawwals, the candles and the mirrors, and grabbed Parul and yanked her up. The music continued to play deafeningly. He dragged her into the car, and she looked apologetically at anyone who caught her eye, as the gossip mill would report the next day.

The parking lot was in an adjacent, empty plot, dusty and dark. Aahan opened the front door of the car and pushed her in. He got into the driver's seat of the car and child locked the vehicle. He began to hit Parul with both hands, and she tried to shield herself with hers. 'Bloody bitch, I'll fix you!' he said repeatedly. A driver from another car walked past nonchalantly. Parul was in shock, and couldn't make a sound, she just tried to defend herself from his blows. The car was stinking. Parul felt something squishy at the base of her foot – she had stepped on some shit while being dragged through the parking lot, it was on the carpeting of the new car now, protective plastic mats hadn't been bought yet.

'You bloody idiot!' roared Aahan, and punched Parul in her right eye. Her eyelid began bleeding, and she screamed in pain. The strains of '*Rang*' wafted into the car, the performance would soon be over.

Aahan snapped out of his blinding rage. 'I'm so sorry baby, I don't know what came over me,' he said, almost in tears. 'I love you so much, and to see you talk to that Bengali buffoon who had you before I did – I just couldn't take it.' He began to kiss her hand.

'I can't go to Masi's like this,' said Parul, in between sobs. Her parents and brother and cousins were in town for the engagement, the house would be full, she was sharing her cousin's room for now, no one could find out. 'I won't go to Sikand House for the first time after our engagement like this.' She sobbed.

They checked into the Grand Hotel for the night. The in-house doctor was called. He examined her indifferently, and prescribed an anti-inflammatory pill and ice pack. Aahan lovingly removed her jewelry and put it on the table. She kept her ring on. He helped her change into the hotel dressing gown and iced her eye, with ice from room service clumsily wrapped into his handkerchief, to reduce the swelling. Nothing could be done about the slight cut on her eyelid. He apologized profusely, kissing her fingertips, and wiped the caked shit from her feet with a wet hand towel. It would never happen again.

A numb Parul said nothing. At this point, it would be so much harder to fight this than to go with it. She wasn't ready to start over. They slept for a couple of hours. She set an alarm for 5 a.m., and Aahan drove her home before everyone awoke.

THREE

BUT, FOR NOW, back again to the party, for Aahan's birthday. Parul went to check on everything in the kitchen. The tandoor was smoking outside the jaali door, doing its bit for Delhi's notoriously bad air quality. The water tanker, which Rajesh's friend had organized, had a white sign on its chipped blue body that read 'Free water for the poor, courtesy Nadeem Miyan, MLC, Sarai Jullena'. Its thick pipe had left a dark trail of water along the driveway into the underground tank. She decided to eat something in case dinner was served too late, a sure sign of the success of the event. Someone had to have their senses about them at the end of the night, to tip the staff, lock up the remaining alcohol.

Candles were lit, the latest blue BMW that they had recently bought was parked conspicuously outside the main gate. Second-hand, dealership test-drive vehicle (Aahan's friend had a friend) but no one needed to know that.

Everyone in their social circle had the latest imported car now, and it was getting difficult to keep changing models so quickly. An hour of waiting and drinking, drinking and waiting later, the guests began to trickle in – their friends, whom they had known since they were children, of whom most had metamorphosed into slightly more refined versions of their parents as they grew up. Undoubtedly, their collective energies, conversations and concerns were no different from those of their parents before them.

Noni, who had been in school with Aahan, worked in some kind of finance job in London, and was one of the few of his friends who had left his family's fold and moved abroad. He had sealed the deal by finding a gori British wife, the kind who wouldn't be considered pretty or smart or rich if she was a desi. But she wasn't, and her British passport and fair-skinned children had compensated that to her husband, in-laws and the world. Noni insisted on inviting Parul's mother-in-law down to the party for a while. He had been fond of her while they were growing up and she had allowed him to stay endless nights and days at the house, playing video games and flaking off with Aahan, an escape from his overachieving professional parents at home, with their impossible and endless expectations. Aahan's mother, who just happened to be sitting in her room, manicured, pedicured, coiffed and in her new Marks & Spencer tunic and tights, instead of smoking in her tie-and-dye nightie with a bandana on her head as usual, walked in to the living room. 'I'll only have a drink with you kids, since Noni is insisting,' she said, and Parul knew that this was the end of any possible enjoyment for her. She started to feel a headache coming on, and wished she was in bed instead, with some dark chocolate and chamomile tea, watching *Downton Abbey*.

'These people just can't be trusted nowadays...' said Mummy, compressing everyone who currently worked as domestic help, anywhere, in whatever role or capacity, or of any caste, religion, region into a single, amorphous entity. It was quite equitable of her, really, Parul thought. Parul had to call her Mummy, and include her in her Mother's Day wishes on Facebook or she would be offended and go into an entirely avoidable sulk. She was in the midst of a group of women who had quite organically settled themselves on the couch while 'the boys' were hovering around the bar. 'Rajesh's father, Laxman, for example,' she continued, as Rajesh poured her whiskey, '... came to this house as a young child. He worked for the Rai Bahadur in exchange for food, his generation was loyal,' she said, gesturing towards the large, ornately framed painting of her father-in-law, looking stern and imposing, above the sofa. 'Today, these boys have turned on their masters, they have forgotten their place. Next they will want to sit on our sofas and eat from the family's plates,' she added, lowering her voice for the last bit rather belatedly for Rajesh's benefit.

'Yes, aunty,' piped in Sonali, a friend of Parul's from her boarding school days, one who had also married into their set, 'my maid goes on leave once a month, you should see how she dresses up for her chutti, jeans and a frilly top from Lajpat Nagar, but can't do anything about her face and hair, can she?' She smiled, a gummy grin, and a bit of paneer hariyali tikka came out and stuck on the side of her mouth but everyone pretended not to notice.

'Yes, beta, my new driver, young chap, just left me in the lurch you know, ran away to the village though I didn't give him leave, he said that his wife was expecting. I couldn't even get a replacement. So inconsiderate, no work ethic,' pronounced Mummy, closing her diatribe against the faceless 'other', those who had let people like her down. Noni's wife was trying to keep up with the bilingual conversation, an omnipresent challenge in a multicultural marriage, but was totally lost at the point when an adult was said to have 'run away' from her hostess's clutches.

Aahan was pretty drunk now, and slipped out of the room, which was full of smoke, perfume, and talk of holiday homes and servants and jewelry and cars and factories and affairs. The noise levels in the room were disorienting him, and he went for a break in the garden, where he rolled himself a joint. He was committed to staying away from the hard stuff, that stuff messed you up for good. He took a deep breath and looked at the foliage around him, twinkling with fairy lights. Delhi smelt of sewage now, all the houses turning into flats and adding more shit into the drains than they were built to handle. His father had dropped by earlier in the evening to wish him a happy birthday, to do his duty as a father. He had been en route to the airport, naturally limiting the time that they could spend together, a relief to both parties. He had brought a gift for Aahan, a steel-grey pin-tuck kurta-pyjama set from a designer store. While it was still in its original packaging, it had clearly been opened, rejected by its original recipient, and then resealed, the tissue paper wrapping noticeably crumpled and torn at places, rewrapped by an amateur. That, along with the fact that it had been in his father's size and not his own, had caused Parul to speculate that it had been recycled by Nooriya at short notice, that his father had, in fact, forgotten that it was his birthday until it was too late to buy a gift. It had hurt Aahan when she had said that, just a twinge, not enough to raise it with her. He looked inside and waved at Rajesh through the glass picture window, forgetting momentarily, in his intoxication, that they were no longer friends.

Waving back, Rajesh continued to man the bar, serving Aahan's friends, who had once allowed him to join in their games and treats, passing the parcel and football and French fries and soft drinks at Aahan's birthday. He was quite relieved that they had slipped into their new, adult roles and that they no longer acknowledged him at any of these events. His invisibility to his former playmates gave him access – they talked about things in front of him that they wouldn't mention around each other, as if he simply wasn't there, still under the archaic notion that the help didn't understand English. Indeed, it was this very misconception that had torpedoed many an affair, soured business deals and relationships between sisters-in-law. The maximum information was usually gleaned by the drivers. All-important conversations, the most lengthy and intimate exchanges routinely and indiscreetly took place in English in the car, idling in traffic, on the mobile phone, and drivers were the silent witnesses to them all. Some had a substantial side income running with blackmail or sale of said information. A driver his cousin knew had financed the reconstruction of his house in the village entirely on this basis, and he didn't even lose his job after. It was bizarre how the sahib-log hadn't caught on to this, simply because they couldn't fathom a world where lower class types spoke the language.

'*Kya loge, Bhaiya?*' he asked one of the guests, with whom he had played kabaddi as a child. He made their drinks extra stiff and watched the results like a television show. Silliness, aggression, bonhomie, silence, would take over them, while Rajesh, who had kept his vow never to drink ever since the incident at the kothi when he was a young boy, enjoyed the temporary and relative advantage his soberness gave him.

'*Woh raat yaad rakhna, Rajesh*,' Madam Aunty had reminded him, as Parul Bhabhi handed him the bar keys earlier that evening. It was a ritual that was followed every time that he had worked the bar at any event at Sikand House. As if he could ever forget.

He had been a teenager, fifteen and a half, and had almost hit his full height of five feet eleven inches. There had been a big party at Sikand House, the roka ceremony of the eldest baby-log, and Madam Aunty and Sahib Uncle had put aside their differences to put up a good show for their daughter's upcoming wedding. The bride-to-be looked like a film star in her blush-pink lehenga, and there were jasmine flowers everywhere. The alcohol was flowing. Rajesh was to remain in the quarter while his parents worked at the event. From his balcony, he had a lateral view of the lawn, and could see his father shadowing Sahib Uncle, securing envelopes and removing stray glasses. The servants' food was delayed, obviously, with such a major event taking priority, and his mother didn't arrive with his dinner at the appointed hour. Bored and a bit hungry, he wandered down from the quarter, to the landing outside the kitchen, into the darkened, empty garage, where the extra bottles of alcohol were stocked, to be taken out if needed. He picked up a green bottle with some kind of bird on the label, he couldn't read the name in the dim light, and impulsively glugged an unknown amount. No one noticed him, and everything seemed all right. It had burnt his throat, tasted awful, but that was about it.

The whiskey had hit him a while later, when he was playing with the dogs, who were tied up near the generator. He started swaying and the world started spinning around him. Terrified, he stumbled into the party, looking for his father to help him. The landscape of the garden had changed for the evening from the familiar space where he and Aahan had played as children. He tripped on a table that he didn't expect, and fell down close to where Madam Aunty was talking to her future samdhan's sister. Madam saw him in her peripheral vision, continued the conversation for a bit, and excused herself. Another servant was swiftly deployed to escort Rajesh to his quarter.

Rajesh's mother had gotten word. She returned to their room, and gave him something to eat, and some water. She had said nothing that night. The next morning, when he woke up, his mouth was dry, his head hurt. His father still wasn't around. He assumed that he must have left for the day with Sahib Uncle. He sat up in bed, disoriented. His mother, unable to contain herself any longer, slapped him twice, once on each cheek.

'*Tumhare wajah se hum beghar ho jayenge! Tumhe pata bhi hai ki tum kitne lucky ho, yahan rehne ki ijjazat hai tumhe?*

Sharab piyo ge? Besharam!' she shouted, followed by a few more spirited slaps placed randomly on his person. Rajesh hid under the bright red and beige velvety razai and waited for his mother's anger to pass. She finished beating him, gave him a banana to eat, along with a glass of lukewarm coconut water, and then left the room to resume her duties.

It was decided that he would write a letter of apology to Madam Aunty and Sahib Uncle. Babita, who had a penchant for theatrics, declared that he would go and read it out in person to the sahib-log to show his sincerity.

Later that evening, completely recovered, he was ushered into the main house. Sahib Uncle was nowhere to be seen, presumably back with that other Nooriya Madam now that the event was over. Madam Aunty and Aahan, the presiding male owing to his father's absence, received him in the TV room upstairs. Aahan looked sympathetic and smirky at the same time. Rajesh's mother nudged him, his father smiled obsequiously. Mortified, he hunched over, attempting to make himself as small as possible, and began to read.

Aadarniye Sahib Uncle aur Madam Aunty,

Didi ki Mangni ke shubh avsar pe maine aapko aur is ghar ko sharminda kiya, is baare me mujhe bahut avsos hai. Mujhe maaf kar dijiye, mein kasam khaata hoon ki aaj ke baad mein sharab kabhi nahin piyoonga.

Aapka,
Rajesh Kumar

The event had gone off well overall, and Madam Aunty was in a good mood. Though she had intended to make an issue out of this, she couldn't help but break into a smile and waved him off. Aahan doubled over laughing.

Rajesh looked down, fixing his gaze on his mother's toe rings, oxidized silver, one a plain band, and another with a snake carved on it. He couldn't get himself to lift his head, it was just too heavy, his mother's toes too compelling. 'Sorry, Madam Aunty' he had wanted to say, but he couldn't get a word out of his mouth, hard as he willed them to come. He walked out of the room, head still lowered, briefly tripping over an ageing Choopey, who yowled indignantly in protest. He never touched alcohol again.

So at the party, Rajesh turned in late, after all the guests had gone, some lingering beyond the host's patience. Parul Bhabhi had asked him to lock up the alcohol to encourage the last of the stragglers to leave. It was difficult for her to handle Aahan's drunk and god-knows-what-else friends, especially after Aahan had himself passed out halfway through the party. After returning the bar key to Bhabhi, and waiting for her to count all the bottles, he ate his dinner, which his mother had left in the kitchen. He heated it in the microwave, and a hot spot in the dal burnt his mouth.

FOUR

THE DAY AFTER his birthday, Aahan woke up with a sore head.

Aahan's father had gone to Dubai, to meet with some buyers, and had left him in charge of the factory. Aahan had suggested several times that he could go meet them himself, that the shop floor wasn't really his scene, but his father was in one of those intermittent tiresome phases – when he felt that his son must learn everything from the ground up – and wouldn't budge.

When Aahan's father had turned twelve, his father before him, Rai Bahadur Sikand, RBS in the business world, had begun grooming him for the automotive parts business. RBS was a wealthy moneylender before Partition, in undivided India, and knew nothing of cars when he arrived in Delhi. An old friend from Peshawar, who he had once helped, was in a position to offer him a contract for shock absorbers, a model of which went into every Hindustan Motors car. The Rai Bahadur spent his own money to host the friend's daughter's wedding in Delhi, and the kanyadaan and doli had been from Sikand House. Not many had a grand home and liquidity in Delhi at that time, and the act of friendship and kindness paid off.

'You can work as hard as you like, but practice cannot teach a besura riyaz. Similarly, business. Entrepreneurship. Risk appetite. These things cannot be taught, they are innate and can only be honed,' RBS had told Aahan's father when he asked to be sent abroad for an MBA. Instead, he had been sent by RBS to bribe a junior officer, who was creating problems.

'I had known nothing of cars in my day,' he would pontificate, and people would listen, because he was rich and powerful. 'All I saw was an opportunity. Business is procuring what you can sell and making a profit on it – simple. My class fellow was in a position to help me, and he knew that I would help him in return. I spent all that I had saved, and even sold my wife's jewels – mind you, she made sacrifices too – and started manufacturing what I could profit on. I even hired a general manager from Detroit, an American called Maurice Johnson, to run the place professionally. It was unthinkable in those days...' he would prattle on, oblivious to the glazed look in the listeners' eyes.

Aahan's father had been easier on his own son. He appreciated the skills he had learnt from his own father, but somewhere resented the tough upbringing that he had had. Anyhow, his multiple personal commitments hadn't allowed him to give Aahan the kind of attention and grooming that his father had given him, which an only son deserved.

Aahan was nowhere near recovered from the previous night, and had had a difficult morning. It was getting more challenging to beat a hangover as he grew older, the body had begun to rebel. At about noon, an Alka-Seltzer, banana-and-peanut-butter toast, coffee, and his wife's and mother's tiresome pep talks and unsolicited advice later, Aahan's driver pulled up at the factory gates in the new Range Rover, the latest one, left at his disposal, and not Nooriya's – it was one of the perks of having his father away. Though he indisputably belonged to that woman, his father was old-fashioned inside, and still liked to think that he was keeping up appearances.

There had been a sea of humanity on the way, some local leader type must be having some bloody meeting and blocking the road.

'*Yeh sab tumhari biradiri key hain, na, Rajesh?*' he said in an accusatory tone to Rajesh, who was sitting in the front seat. He had stayed the night at Sikand House after bartending at the party, and needed to be at the industrial area in the morning. His father had left earlier with the scooter, and Rajesh had waited by the car in the driveway for Aahan to arrive and asked him for a lift.

'*Bas pahunch hi rahen hain, Bhaiya*,' Rajesh reassured him mechanically, distracted. He was looking at the turnout for the rally, his reason for visiting the industrial area. Scores of men were arriving in the back of open trucks, holding on tenaciously to whatever they could for support. There was a bottleneck ahead. A chota Vikram with hundreds of dusty cases of packaged water in single-serve plastic glasses as its cargo had stalled apologetically, halving the width of the road. The Range Rover managed to squeeze past, all possible alarm sounds beeping. They weren't designed for the coziness of Indian roads, where cars and humans often came close not just because they had to, but simply because they could, quite like they did when lining up for anything, as if coming that inch closer would make them reach their destination any faster.

'As if the roads weren't bad enough. These people are so inconsiderate. I'm hungover as it is, and now this,' Rajesh heard Aahan whine on the phone, presumably to Bhabhi.

They arrived at the entrance of Sikand Automotives and the security guard opened the motorized gates for the Range Rover, its glossy black exterior covered in a generous film of dust.

'Good Morning, Baba!' Rajesh's father, Laxman Chacha, called out, smiling and bending slightly. He was waiting for him at the lobby with a sheaf of papers. Aahan rolled his eyes and tried to swallow, but his mouth was parched. The old man had been nipping at his heels to look at some paperwork for the last couple of days, in his annoyingly over-sincere manner.

'For god's sake, I am thirty-two years old and the father of a child,' Aahan thought to himself, and made a mental note to start calling him Laxman Kumar now that he was older, hoping to nudge him towards reciprocating with an equally appropriate title.

He entered the building, not acknowledging anyone, he was just too tired and hot and bothered, and went straight to his father's cabin, locked the door, made himself a Nespresso and lit a joint. He sat down, and imbibed both, coffee first, and began to relax. He decided to watch a few of the torrents that he had downloaded onto his laptop before he approached the day.

It was lunch hour at the factory, and as old Mr Sikand was away, Laxman Chacha – as he was known to everyone now – would allow them the entire hour off, instead of the fifteen-minute shifts they would otherwise eat in. Baba wouldn't even notice. As soon as the bell rang, the workers ate quickly, the rice, dal, achaar and onion fragrances mixing with the smell of sweat seamlessly to produce what Aahan's oldest sister had named 'the Indian smell' on her visit to the inauguration of the new cafeteria years ago.

They were in a hurry today, spending less time than usual on gossip and cards. Aahan didn't check production targets every day, and the staff knew it. They were in a rush, because Manoj Bhai was going to be speaking today at the rally. Now, normally this would have been of some interest, but there would hardly be a fire under their asses to go and listen. But Rajesh was one of the organizers, and he had offered each of them 300 rupees and a quarter bottle of Director's Cut whiskey if they showed up, even for an hour, just for Manoj Bhai's speech.

Rajesh, who often dropped his father on the scooter to the factory in the mornings and picked him up in the evenings so that he could have use of the vehicle during the day, was popular with everyone and happy to help with all his 'connections'. Whether his father knew what he was up to or not was a subject of some debate, but anyhow the guard turned a blind eye when scores of them left the premises and walked over in the blinding sunlight to a park nearby, where the meeting was to be held.

Rajesh stood proudly on the podium, just behind all the leader-log. Manoj Bhai, his political mentor, was to make a speech today, and Rajesh had to introduce him, with a short speech to warm the crowd up – a nod by the leader to his growing stature in the party ecosystem. He had practiced his lines in front of the mirror that morning, with his mother hovering outside, trying to listen in through a crack in the thin plywood door, demanding to know what he was doing.

'*Mere pyare bhaiyon aur behenon, ab manch pe maujood hai woh! Hamare dardon ko samajhne wala, hamari aawaz duniya tak pahaunchne wala, har ma ka beta, har behen ka bhai, har mazdoor ki asha hai woh. Police ki permanent naukri chhod kar nyay ke liye ladne wala, hamare apna Manoj Bhai, ab kuch lafz bolenge*,' he told his reflection, trying to ignore the sounds just outside.

Manoj Bhai was unexceptional in his looks, a lab specimen of the North Indian male, aside from his eyes – the right one had failed to develop any colour, and remained red-and-white like a rabbit's. The labour leader had originally been a constable, but years of witnessing repeated beatings, sexual assault and extortion from close quarters, which were usually settled for fee or favour anyway, had worn him down. The final nail in the coffin of his police career was rumoured to have been when a youth he had booked for stalking a girl in his neighbourhood – whom he had known since she was a child – and for throwing acid on her face, had gotten off with a light punishment by furnishing a fake birth certificate, pretending to be a minor, through bribery and influence. Along with police work, he had given up his last name years ago, in a bid to fight caste injustice. He was now known simply as Manoj Bhai or 'Manoj Bhaisaheb' to the particularly deferent.

Rajesh gave a satisfied grin when he noticed the blue-and-beige uniforms, which he had grown up seeing, trickle into the ground. His quota was going to be complete. There were nearly four hundred workers from the entire industrial area present. There was the contingent from the Sikand factory, the Kasais from the buffalo factory and a smattering of white people – interns at the technology conglomerate, who had taken to eating lunch at the shop floor and had come to support their colleagues. Rajesh was sure that the goras would be counted as a special success, and was momentarily annoyed at the good luck of whoever had recruited them. The crowd had largely been treating the rally thus far as a social occasion to catch up with their relatives, who worked in the different factories. Three of Rajesh's own cousins and cousins-in-law were in the gathering too.

Rajesh took the mike, and looked around. He had a bird's-eye view of the park.

'*Kaafi public hai*,' he thought to himself, nervously. 'Hello, hello, check 1-2-3. Hello, hello, mike check,' he began, hesitantly.

The crowd continued with their socializing, oblivious to Rajesh's plea for attention.

Rajesh forgot all his lines, and continued repeating, 'Check 1-2-3, check 1-2-3,' to the now attentive and bemused audience, until Manoj Bhai came up to him, put his arm around him, and said into the mike, '*Haan ji, beta, chal raha hai* mike,' jovially to Rajesh.

The crowd roared with laughter. Rajesh came out of his trance, mortified. Manoj Bhai gestured with his eyes for Rajesh to move aside, and began his speech.

'My brothers, you have sacrificed a lot to come here today, expecting nothing in return. It is this sacrifice that you make every day, in little ways, whether it is giving up your lunch break to come and see me, or it is taking an extra shift when your colleague's wife is unwell so that he doesn't lose pay,' he began. 'But what is this life of yours? The life of a beast of burden. You work, you pay, you toil as long as there is breath in your body, then you die. You smile and salute the factory owner as you get off from your second-hand scooter and he gets out of his badi gaadi, and hope he keeps your izzat by acknowledging you. Sometimes he does, sometimes he doesn't. Your children study in government schools, his in private schools. But the worst is when your children are ill, and you cannot care for them, because you don't have money or time. If his children are ill, he will not come to the factory. If his wife has a puja at home, he will not come. If his cousin's daughter gets married, he won't come to the factory. But you? If you miss even a day, for any reason, you risk losing your wages or even your job. Why? I ask you why? Why you? It is because he is the one who is useless! He has got this factory from his baap-dada and you are the one actually running it. It cannot go on without you. So I implore you, go into your workplaces and demand better pay, demand health insurance, demand sick leave. Because it is he who cannot do without you, not the other way around. Show him the power of our numbers.'

Parts of the crowd, as if on cue, applauded enthusiastically and shouted slogans; the ones who hadn't been briefed adequately continued to chat.

Rajesh was numb with shame, unable to speak, or even look at any one. He had skulked off the podium in ignominy, and squatted down on the dusty ground just behind the structure. He had blown it. Manoj Bhai's words, booming from the speaker just adjacent to where he sat, played in his mind like muzak, and had their intended effect of triggering memories of his own past childhood humiliations.

As an only child, aside from the somewhat unequal, and later sporadic companionship of Aahan, Rajesh had spent most of his growing years around adults, the men and women who worked at Sikand House. As servant in status, if without any duties, at least in the early days, he experienced the sort of thing that Manoj Bhai was talking about constantly. Like the other servants, those wishing to have a peaceful life in any event, he had learnt to treat it like a chronic disease, like diabetes or an ulcer, to be managed or tolerated, but one that he was constantly aware of, nevertheless.

While he did go to a good school, he wasn't ever allowed to have any friends over because of the no-visitors rule for servants. Aahan was often away with playdates and classes, or had his friends over, and Rajesh wasn't asked to join. In fact, he preferred being left out, as opposed to Aahan's birthdays, when he had to join in, no matter what. He had refused to wear Aahan's hand-me-downs for the event since he was about eight, forcing his parents to buy him a new outfit from Sarojini Nagar market every year, which he would repeat on his own birthday the following year. His parents agreed to many such demands, but drew the line on a new school bag at the start of every school year; he would have to make do with what Aahan discarded, no matter if the featured cartoon characters weren't his favourite.

Aahan was in a different school, it would be like new, they reasoned. There was everything a child could want at Aahan's birthday, and Rajesh would have to experience it alone, as none of the other children would play with him. Divya, Aahan's sister, would approach him, ask him if he was having fun, but he was intimidated by her gaggle of girlfriends, older girls with long legs and easy laughs. He would avoid her when her friends were around, though he very much wanted to talk to her. Most of the kids at the party were only mildly interested in the toys and games on offer, attending an event like this was a regular thing for them. The khoi bag was the equalizer, with children of fixers and bureaucrats and a servant pushing and vying together for the same cheap tat.

All rules were suspended for those three or four minutes after the birthday boy broke the piñata, and Rajesh would attack it enthusiastically, pushing aside Aahan's friends, and examining his loot in his room later with a sense of accomplishment.

Very early on, he had decided that he wasn't cut out for a life of service. Simple everyday humiliations affected him in a way that they didn't seem to affect the adult servants. They laughed it off with a crude joke here and there, and didn't appear to give it a second thought. Ice and cold water was precious in those days, with the household having a small, single fridge, the contents of which were reserved for the Sikand family. It wasn't for servants, even in the height of summer, and they had to make do with water from a matka kept outside the kitchen. But family members would let it sit and get warm instead of gulping it down immediately. His not being allowed to sit on the sofa while the lazy, hairy family dogs could sleep on it all day. Not being allowed to access the house and play when Aahan or his sisters had friends over, though they did send over some leftover snacks for him to the quarter, sweet and savoury all mashed together in a steel plate, after the friends had left. He balked at how his father would endure harsh words from Aahan's teenaged sister, whom he had dropped to nursery school when they were little. He wasn't encouraged to interact with these older girls as a servant child of the opposite gender. If he had a sister, she would probably have been conscripted into being a lady in waiting for them.

He always resented how they had to skulk around the property, attempting to make themselves invisible, as if the very sight of them would sully the landscape. They didn't exist in the house except to serve. Gardening was his hobby, but once his proficiency was discovered, he was put to work to assist the maali in the evenings, after he had finished his homework, against his wishes. The sahib-log owned his skill as long as he lived there, and it was presented as a favour to him on top of it. '*Kuch seekh jayega, Laxman, aage kaam ayega*,' Madam Aunty had told his ever-smiling father.

Rebellion of any kind was not an option. If he had made a nuisance of himself, Madam Aunty would simply send him and his mother away, and in the worst case, his father too, with no warning or notice period, though this was unlikely. His father's pre-eminent position as head servant meant that there were many others who wanted him out, and tried to trip him up on a daily basis, and weren't above using Rajesh or his mother to make this happen. Petty squabbles reigned, with the sahib-log oblivious to the goings-on. Missing eggs, disproportionate washing powder consumption, inflated petrol bills, were often implied, and sometimes openly alleged.

Rajesh had thrived in the politically charged atmosphere, and became his parents' eyes and ears, his gardening duties offering him more access across the property than he would have otherwise had. He would report bits of information that he gleaned while watering the plants on the main house balconies to his parents, raw data – he wasn't sure how they could use it.

Towards this end, he had no qualms using Aahan. While the distance between them had grown, he knew his nature viscerally, and had decided that the best strategy would be to keep this card for a big one, and not fetter it away on the usual daily fights, in which he knew Aahan would have no interest or empathy, having never experienced this kind of pettiness over day-to-day survival in his own life.

When Rajesh was sixteen, a fight had been brewing between his father and Babloo, the son of a family retainer from Madam Aunty's family, the nephew of her childhood cook from her maika. As Sahib Uncle had been spending most of his time away from Sikand House, with Nooriya Madam, Aahan's mother was looking at getting more people loyal to her, from her family, into her employment. She was suspicious of everyone, and embarrassed of what they knew, especially Laxman Kumar, who accompanied her husband everywhere, and presumably knew all his secrets. His father was in a difficult position. While he respected the first Madam as the rightful wife of Sahib, he knew that if he didn't do Nooriya Madam's bidding, he would be out on the street in a day. Babloo was spending more time in the kothi and Laxman out of it with Sahib; it was rumoured that he would be getting family housing too, Rajesh had heard Madam Aunty talk about it on the phone one evening, when he was watering the plants on the balcony outside her bedroom.

That just wouldn't do, resources were already too strained in the quarters. There was always a long wait for the use of the common bathroom. There was no extra space to dry the clothes his mother hurriedly washed in her limited bathroom time. His mattress in the balcony alcove had to be rolled up during the day, with the clothes drying on a line above.

Babita, Laxman and Rajesh had decided as a family that they needed to get Babloo out, and a plan was hatched. Babita, who had the additional charge of caring for Madam Aunty's clothes, had swiped her underwear and a thick, red glass bangle from her room. Madam Aunty's trust in the system and inability to look into detail was so pronounced that she hadn't noticed. This was expected and planned for. The lost items were placed in Babloo's room when he wasn't around, in a place that he wouldn't look at in a hurry, to be discovered at an opportune time.

The time to strike came soon enough. One winter morning, Rajesh had spotted Aahan behind the servant quarter wall, where passersby came to pee, smoking an adolescent cigarette, not really inhaling it though, because he hated it and didn't know how in those days anyway. He came down the narrow spiral staircase outside his parents' room, and joined him. Aahan looked at him and nodded, but didn't say anything. Rajesh asked him for a cigarette too. Aahan obliged; he lit up, and they smoked half the cigarette together in silence.

As Aahan was throwing away the remains, Rajesh had said to him: 'You are my elder brother so I am telling you this. Have Babloo's room searched. He has bad intentions for Madam Aunty. He is reporting to someone else.'

Meanwhile, Babloo had seen the duo smoke together; the servant areas were too cramped for him to have missed it. He was as keen to have Laxman's family removed from the premises as in the reverse. He immediately went to Madamji to tell her that Rajesh was corrupting Aahan, teaching him to smoke. Accusations flew; Aahan listened quietly. Though he was a teenager, he was the alpha male of the house with his father's frequent absences. He commanded Laxman Kumar to search Babloo's room in his presence. Babloo couldn't say anything to the man-child with a fuzzy upper lip. Anyway, he had nothing to hide – or so he thought.

After an elaborate charade of ransacking the room, Aahan saw his mother's underpants and bangle emerge from a crumpled plastic bag in a dusty dark corner under the charpoy. Naturally, Babloo's cries of innocence went unheard, and he was never seen at Sikand House again.

As they graduated from school, Aahan was sent off to study management in Australia. The US dollar was strong, and though he was still quite well off, Aahan's father was stretched a bit thin for cash, having to run two establishments, and factor in costs for the wedding of Divya, his daughter who was still unmarried, unsettled.

Though still a child, there was also Aman, his son with Nooriya, to think of. When the time came, he knew that he wouldn't get off cheap from that situation. Australia was relatively less expensive than England or America for education and cost of living. The girls had studied in Delhi, and there was no shame in that. But his son, he must be sent abroad, it was the done thing. Besides, unlike his daughters, who had done well enough in their Board exams to secure places in half-decent girls' colleges at Delhi University, his son had performed abominably, and had done so by design, to ensure that he could leave. No college in India, where he would have deigned to go, would have him, and this arrangement suited him just fine.

Rajesh had wanted out, too, but his options were more limited. He couldn't live at the kothi anymore, outside his parents' room, on a rolled-up mattress. He had done his time there, and he wanted his life to begin. Aahan's father, Sahib Uncle, had agreed to pay his college and hostel fees at Delhi University. It was heavily subsidized by the government, and was a paltry amount for him, but life-changing for Rajesh.

'It's at the price of a couple of dinners out, and the boy will be gone, and I don't want a young man living there with no purpose. Aahan is leaving too, there will be just ladies in the house,' Laxman had heard him justify to Nooriya. Aahan's mother didn't care as much about where he spent what – as long as she, her children and her household were well cared for – possibly because of her comparative security in the situation. Rajesh wasn't bothered about what course he studied, and where he went, as long as it was away.

Rajesh passed his exams, and managed to secure a place at Kanti College, Hindi Honours (evening). Then there was the question of a hostel room, he had to have a hostel room. Though these were usually hard to come by, with them being reserved for out-of-town students, Aahan's father used a contact in the university, enrolling him with his village address, his great-grandfather's old house at Chakia, a place he had been to twice in his life. He was, on paper, from Bihar now, like many of his other classmates.

The college hostel was bleak. The university didn't have money to spend on frills. It was in keeping with the prevalent Indian notion that suffering was somehow noble, and there was an unwritten, un-institutionalized, yet cohesive effort on the part of all those who worked at these places to go that extra mile to make them as uncomfortable as they could. The rooms, like many in the city, were not weatherproof: they were unbearably hot in the summer, and there was seepage in even the best of the rooms during the monsoon months. The worst ones, usually to be shared by the freshers, required buckets to be permanently stationed under leaky parts, which could be located as inconveniently as over the beds. The end of the monsoon meant a swarm of mosquitoes from the stagnant water everywhere by mid-September. After a few bearable, albeit smoggy, weeks after Diwali, the small, dark and airless rooms would be freezing. Students were not allowed heaters because the frayed wires of the building couldn't take the electrical load.

When Babita had asked the warden if she could give her beloved son a rod heater for the winter, she was patronizingly told that it was a hostel, not a hotel, and that it seemed liked she had removed the letter S from the word. This was a pun quite lost on the unlettered woman, but the warden was quite proud of it and resolved to use it again on any parents who made unreasonable demands.

Rajesh was to earn his own expenses and, again, Sikand Uncle's largesse helped him get a job at the brand-new McDonalds, which had opened in Kamla Nagar market, close to the university. He was to work there in the mornings and attend classes in the evening, and hopefully become the first college graduate in his family. One of his cousins was already twelfth-pass, denying him that honour.

He left Sikand House early one humid, oppressive, July morning, when the monsoon hadn't broken. His VIP suitcase, an old one of Madam Aunty's, had been packed, full of the new clothes he had splurged on at the Sarojini Nagar market, with the money given to him by his father. Unlike on the day when he came into this world, and into Sikand House, Aahan's father had allowed Laxman Kumar the use of one of the family vehicles – the old Maruti Esteem, which was now the 'sabzi car', used to run errands by staff without the family present – to drop him off at the university. It was understood that going forward, while he was permitted to visit his parents, even stay for a night or two, that he was never to live there again. Babita, who had a penchant for drama, cried copious tears, which she ostentatiously wiped on her dupatta at regular intervals. She had given up on wearing sarees years ago, with deference to her ever-expanding girth. She did a puja for him at the wall-mounted altar in their room, and he stood beside her, embarrassed, impatient and just a little bit emotional. Dahi was mixed with sugar and he was force-fed a bite before he was ready to leave.

No one had come from the Sikand family to bid him farewell – 9.00 a.m. was just too early. Instead, he had been summoned up to the main house by Sahib Uncle the previous evening, Madam Aunty had also been there. Rajesh had thanked them for all they had done for him, touched their feet, accepted an envelope with one thousand and one rupees, and he was off.

Aahan had left earlier that year. There had been a long gap between the end of his school life and the start of his college term in Australia, and his father had been keen that he begin coming into the office to learn the ropes a bit. He knew that the boy had to be groomed, disciplined, and he was willing to endure Nooriya's wrath to get that going. Aahan, instead, implored his father to let him have a few months of vacation time before he started his business degree; he was so tired. Aahan's father had always been vaguely guilty of his second family and the impact that it had on the first, and capitulated quickly. In any event, his absence from the office for a bit longer, delaying the inevitable though it was, would mean peace in the immediate future with Nooriya, and three months wouldn't change the course of history. Aahan was sent abroad on a long holiday before his course started, visiting his friends who were already studying at colleges in England and America. The whole house was involved in the preparations for his departure. As he was going to be living in self-catering accommodation, the chef was instructed to teach him basic cooking. He got as far as boiling an egg and making a cheese toast. The entire kitchen staff stood and watched, giggling ever so slightly, at him attempting to slice an apple. He had never eaten a fruit whole, without it being pre-plated, and didn't want to start now. When he cut his finger slightly, Babita swooped in and took over, proclaiming that she just couldn't see Baba like this. It was hot in the kitchen, and this project was quickly abandoned. Ready meals, which he could heat in the microwave, were packed and a set of new Samsonite suitcases was bought.

The morning that Aahan was to leave, the household was bustling. His bags were carried down the stairs from his room at the top of the house, and fitted into the car in different permutations, as directed by Laxman. When the boot just wouldn't shut, one bag was put on the front seat, with an old bedsheet protecting the cream leather upholstery. Pudin Hara hadn't been packed by mistake, and a driver was dispatched hurriedly to the local chemist to buy multiple strips; it wouldn't be available abroad. His favourite breakfast, an elaborate south Indian feast, idli, dosa, vada, chutney and filter coffee was prepared – his last meal at home before his departure. Divya had wanted a cup of tea, but had to make it herself with a tea bag, because no one from the staff was available to assist her. Aahan's mother was teary and had declared that she would drop him to the airport. She had tried to arrange a pass to stay with him at the airport until he boarded the flight, but this idea was firmly rejected by him.

The day of his departure had also been his half-brother, Nooriya's son's, birthday, so his father was absent when he left.

FIVE

AAHAN'S FATHER HAD a secret, albeit a terribly kept one. Many years ago, when his wife began to lose her looks – all fat and drooped and stretched with age and time and repeated childbirth and miscarriages – he began to actively seek a lover. His parents were dead, and hers had lost everything years ago, causing her father to die suddenly from a heart attack. All that she was to bring to the table had not materialized. Her brother had excluded her and kept what was left, leaving her old mother for her to care for as her inheritance. He couldn't do away with her, and neither did he want to, the system worked overall. But he needed sex and adulation, neither of which was forthcoming from his increasingly self-involved and disinterested wife. Initially, he began visiting prostitutes, just occasionally, to let off some steam – painfully young girls with vacant eyes who let him fuck them in seedy hotel rooms. But that wasn't to his taste.

He needed companionship just as much as he needed sex, but the unquestioning, adoring type. He wanted to get the right mistress, so that it wouldn't end up being a hassle. He knew of many people who had gone down this path, where initially everything was all rosy, but ultimately, on balance, there was double the bother and half the satisfaction.

Mr and Mrs Sikand went to cocktail parties nearly every night in those days, they were quite the rage back in the 1980s. The women wore diaphanous sarees, and the men mostly sported innocently ridiculous three-piece suits, save the occasional neta's son in a crisp white kurta-pyjama. Initially he would go everywhere with his wife, opening the car door for her, keeping his arm around her protectively if any man spoke to her. She started enjoying gin and tonics in the day and whiskey at night. Soon, she enjoyed them too much and he let her be, chatting with the younger, perkier women, whilst their husbands protectively put their arms around them. His wife always seemed to be on some diet or the other, but it never helped. Alcohol without food didn't suit her, and she would get quickly drunk and everyone would get uncomfortable. Slowly, they started socializing separately, asking fewer and fewer questions of each other.

At one such event, hosted by an acquaintance in the neighbourhood, he came across the perfect woman. She was a divorcée, he learnt through the grapevine. The candidate had the schooling and the manners and the accent, which were very important to him – he couldn't be with a dehat or a cow, however attractive. In an all-too-familiar pattern, she had left her husband, and had then been rejected by her parents, worried that she would stake a claim to her brothers' property. A number of theories swirled around as to why and there were murmurs that her ex-husband was gay or impotent or both. She now lived in a tiny barsati in Defence Colony, with her beloved Alsatian, unsuited as the poor chap was for Delhi in general and barsatis specifically. She lived alone, hadn't any children that anyone had seen or heard of, and her body had maintained its shape and youthfulness that women of that generation lost so quickly with childbearing. She worked as an interior designer, commuting to and from her office by auto-rickshaw every morning and evening, the dust irritating her eyes and the bumpiness rattling her spine. Earlier, she must have had a car and driver to take her wherever she wished, and Aahan's father speculated that her ex-husband must have done something terrible to her to make her go through this inconvenience, which in all likelihood meant that her expectations were likely to be pretty low.

He got talking to her while they were both waiting to use the bathroom, in the guest room, its walls decorated with life-size portraits of the host's family, eerily grinning down at them. They spoke of the weather, about the difficulties of getting a car allotted – there was such a long waitlist. She had been waiting over six months for a Fiat, she had selected a mint-green colour.

'I am in the automotives business. Perhaps I can help?' he said, but she didn't accept his generous offer. His turn came first, and he waited outside the bathroom for her, even though he had finished, and they returned to the party in the living room together.

'I picked up smoking while I studied in Rome, when I was a teenager,' she told him, as she took a puff on her cigarette. 'Dirty habit, but then I don't have a husband to answer to.' She pushed back her chin-length hair. She had grown up all over the world, she said, her father had been a foreign service officer and was retired now. She regaled him with stories of a childhood spent in Zamalek and Clifton and Trastevere. He relaxed in her company, aware as he was of his wife watching him from the corner of her eye from across the room.

All this international exposure had honed her sense of design, she said, and she worked at an architect's office as an interior designer. Aahan's father vaguely knew him.

'Isn't your office on the way to my factory?' he said, and offered to pick her up and drop her back every day, just until she got her car. 'I cannot see a lady suffer!' he proclaimed grandly, as she gave him her visiting card.

Aahan's mother joined the conversation, staggering just a little. She had skipped dinner in yet another bid to lose weight, and the whiskey had made her lightheaded quicker than she thought it would. She needed to end this night now. She held on to her husband's arm for support and introductions were made. '*Chalien?*' she said to her husband, tightly.

The first day he was to pick her up, he examined himself in the mirror attached to his wife's dressing table, and sucked in his gut. He wore a better shirt than usual and set off on his mission. He would henceforth only let Laxman drive him to and fro from work, no one else could be trusted to be discreet. Getting into the rear seat for the short ride to the address that Nooriya had given him, he waited, lighting a cigarette while

Laxman went up the narrow staircase of her barsati to ring the bell. She came down in a chiffon saree and a sleeveless blouse, and slid in beside him. He took out another cigarette, lit it with the burning tip of his own, and handed it to her. She accepted it, taking it to her lips.

Her upbringing in a diplomatic household showed. The conversation always flowed, the ride always ended too quickly. She got off at her workplace and he appreciated her derriere as she exited the vehicle. He was willing to be patient; it was part of the excitement.

Seasons changed, and she started wearing a brightly coloured ikat coat over her sari. One Friday morning, she was already waiting outside the gate when he pulled up. He hadn't any time to light a cigarette for her. She sat beside him, plucked his cigarette from his fingers, took a deep drag, and returned it. Her lipstick left a mark, and was a bit sticky when Aahan's father took it to his lips.

That evening, when he was dropping her back, he asked her if he could come up to her flat to use the telephone. He had forgotten some important files in the office and would need to call in to have them collected. Could he possibly wait at her house while Laxman rushed back to collect them – it was really urgent. Of course he could! Would he like a coffee? Or something a bit stronger? She had a bottle of whiskey that she had received as a present on her birthday. Yes, why not, it had been a hard day, the weekend is upon us. She took out the whiskey and two glasses. Laxman had been told to take his time. He told her about his marriage; how it had been arranged at a young age and how they lived separate lives, together just for the children. She touched his arm in sympathy. He kissed her gently, the taste of whiskey still in her mouth. After that, he would come over after work every day.

Laxman sensed the change in the conversation in the car, her giggles as he touched her between her legs in the back seat like a teenager, but said nothing. Sikand Sahib was good to him, and it wasn't his business. He waited outside her house while the Sahib had her, but told no one, not even his wife. Soon, the new couple would get dropped off at her house, after work, and Sahib would tell Laxman to leave the car behind and to go ahead, to take the bus, and he did as he was told. Everyone saw Sahib return home at 6.30 a.m., before his family woke up, but no one said anything, to him that is.

Aahan's father improved Nooriya's living standards, he installed an air conditioner in the barsati, paid for a new television. It smelt of smoke, and the furnishings were covered in dog hair, but he didn't care. He suggested moving the other woman to an apartment he owned, closer to the factory, but she refused. She just wanted him, not his money, she said. He stopped coming home at all for days on end, and she added a cupboard for his things in her bedroom. 'She consumed him, kha gayi ussey,' people would say when they discussed the affair.

Aahan's mother outwardly carried on as if nothing had happened. Men did this. Her late father and father-in-law both had mistresses at some point, but had died by their wives' sides. Even her idiot brother was carrying on with a neighbour in Calgary. She would just have to wait it out. Could be weeks, months, or possibly even years, but it would end.

Her hair began to fall. Just a little at first – she would notice a few extra strands on her pillow when she woke up, alone. As the months passed, the drain would be clogged with clumps of her long, black hair when she washed it. She began to collect it obsessively, saving it in a musical jewelry box that the Rai Bahadur had bought for her as a gift on a trip to Vienna, when she was a young bride. It would play 'Eine kleine Nachtmusik' as she organized the strands, tying them into neat bundles with colourful rubber bands saved from the newspaper. It was at this time, and this time alone, that she allowed herself to sob – a controlled explosion. She scheduled this after a bath, and before she put on her eye makeup, or it would be smudged.

'Why don't you say something to him, Mamma?' raged her daughter, Divya.

'You are old enough to see what is going on, beta, but not wise enough to understand its implications,' she replied, and refused to discuss the matter any further.

Divya took to repeatedly calling Nooriya's number and hanging up when her father was with her, until they would put the phone off the hook.

Aahan's mother cut her remaining hair short, till her chin. The lack of weight made it frizz up, looking even shorter than it was. On the few evenings her husband did come home, he slept in the guest bedroom. They interacted primarily in the company of their children, or were always waited on by their servants, with no real opportunity for confrontation – a relief for him. If he noticed his wife's thinning hair, he didn't comment on it.

She went to an ayurvedic hair-care centre, run by a widow with a home in a posh neighbourhood, to meet her expenses. The establishment functioned from the widow's living room, and was staffed by her old family retainers – cheerful, efficient women in brightly coloured, expertly tied sarees. They would, under her supervision, apply traditional hair packs onto clients, women only, tailored to their hair concerns, and to be washed off under the sink of the guest bedroom on the ground floor. The house would be full of assorted ladies at any given time, a community bound together by the desire for better hair.

Many of Maha-Maharajji's followers frequented this establishment, and the proprietress had even framed a picture of the godman, with his signature open palm namaste, to make them more comfortable. Shying away from their smirks, real or imagined, Aahan's mother stopped going.

Nooriya, like many mistresses before her, had time on her hands most evenings. It was difficult for her to tolerate that her man had another family, a legitimate one, that she could not refer to their relationship openly, that a simple outing to a restaurant was not possible for them. The relationship that was her everything did not exist outside the four walls of the barsati.

Nooriya took to accompanying her recently widowed cousin, her Mama's daughter, who had grown children and long empty evenings, to Maha-Maharajji ka ashram, on some of the evenings when she was alone, when he was with his wife and children. She had found Maha-Maharajji to be luminous.

He had looked at her and drawn an invisible sindoor with his thumb where her hair parted, and sent her along wordlessly.

The evenings were the hardest to pass, when other women her age were busy with homework and infants and husbands and mothers-in-law. Dusk was the hour of self-reflection, which both of them were united in their desire to avoid. Her cousin would pick her up in her ink-blue Premier Padmini, and take her rumbling across town to the ashram, a non-descript, cream-coloured building in a sprawling complex on the outskirts of the city.

No one knew quite how Maha-Maharajji had managed to annex this large piece of land; it was one of his many miracles. They became sevadaars, helping with the langar, manning the shoe counter, giving out tokens for footwear left behind for safekeeping by devotees, and attending Maha-Maharajji's discourses.

'I welcome followers of all faiths. Hindu-Muslim-Sikh-Isahi, it doesn't matter to me. Lost souls of any religion, any caste will naturally find me,' he had said in the very first pravachan that Nooriya attended. 'I encourage each of you to follow your own god, whoever or wherever he or she is,' he urged. 'Can you see him?' he asked, and then held his mike to the crowd.

'Yes!' They roared in unison.

Not committed enough to be in the inner circle – yet regular enough though that Maha-Maharajji now recognized her and greeted her in the distinctive open palm namaste that he reserved for the staunch believers – Nooriya became pally with some of the women who frequented the ashram, and she quickly learnt about the ashram cliques, who was in one camp or the other. They came in shifts. The women with young, school-going children usually came in the late mornings and had their own group. This time was also popular with older, retired men. Afternoons were slow and evenings, the time that she usually came, were older women, with children who didn't need them, a minuscule fraction of single, working women like herself, and the few men who were either exceptionally devout followers of Maha-Maharajji or dragged there by their wives to atone for some indiscretion or the other.

She would come to the ashram a few times a week, lingering on after her seva to chat with the stragglers, hoping for a darshan. Maha-Maharajji was keen on building a community and didn't discourage this practice. She discovered that a number of women from the Sikands' social circle came to the ashram. A natural listener, she gave them the attention that they didn't get from their husbands and children. Soon, she was being invited to their homes for their cocktail parties.

It was a matter of time before she ran into Aahan's mother.

The event where they met was an otherwise predictable affair, a cocktail party. The usual drill, a birthday, copious rum, whiskey and tandoori snacks, no dinner was to be served. Aahan's mother saw Nooriya almost immediately upon entering, and froze. Having gone straight from her father's home to her husband's, she had little experience with territorial confrontation. Her mother-in-law had passed away early, and so she had the run of a large establishment pretty quickly. There was no one to call out her mistakes. Her parents were now dead, and her husband was otherwise occupied, he couldn't care less what she got up to, as long as she left him to live his life in peace. Her children were too young, and she had never entered the workplace. The lack of scrutiny by anyone also meant that she had let herself go. Her jowls drooped, and her blouses were a bit tight – she had to have them opened out. She had a disproportionately large tummy as compared to her torso. Her breasts sagged noticeably from feeding her babies, and the stretch marks from carrying them made her tie her saris higher. All that had remained desirable about her was her milky white skin, and she took great pains to protect it from the sun.

In contrast, Nooriya had a honey-brown complexion, an hourglass figure with her saree tied below her belly button, and possessed the confidence of a woman who had made her own way in the world, who didn't have to answer to anyone, who had her man where she wanted him.

Aahan's father wasn't there, he was travelling on business. Nooriya was heady with his devotion. Aahan's mother, facing the humiliation of rejection, both by her husband, and by her friend who had invited them both, took a deep breath and a big gulp of her drink. The drawing room grew crowded, even claustrophobic. Inevitably, Nooriya and Aahan's mother came face to face. Aahan's mother had conducted many imaginary conversations on lonely nights leading up to this moment.

Nooriya looked her up and down, and said, 'Oh hello there, we've met before. We have your husband in common.' She blew a smoke ring nonchalantly.

Speechless, Aahan's mother left the room, walked over to the street in the dark, continued until she found Laxman smoking a bidi under a tree and went back home.

The hostess for the evening, who had been watching this from the corner of her eye, was simultaneously relieved and disappointed. On one hand, there had been no scene. On the other hand, there had been no scene. Nooriya had emerged the clear winner without firing a single shot – it had to be Maha-Maharajji's blessings, she concluded. She went and put her arm around Nooriya and asked her if she would like another drink.

What they say about first impressions is true. They do set the tone for an equation, one that can only be undone with a change in circumstances. After her first defeat, Aahan's mother could not recover the ground that she had lost. She had shown her hand, revealed her naked fear of the younger, more confident woman, for all to see. The news spread like wildfire, and to ride out the storm, Aahan's mother began to spend even more time at home. When she did go out, she drank quickly and unpleasantly. The invitations began to dry up. Those who visited her reported that Nooriya was an integral part of the Maha-Maharajji set now.

Aahan's father had heard about 'the face-off that wasn't' from Nooriya. She reported it factually. He didn't bring it up, didn't say anything to anyone, nothing had happened, really. If he saw his wife's discomfiture, he thought it best to let it pass, spending more and more evenings with Nooriya, either in her bed, or out with her at the homes of the Maha-Maharajji bunch. They came to be accepted in that society as a de facto couple, and Aahan's mother retreated into Sikand House, with just a few old friends visiting from time to time, on their way to cocktail parties.

One such evening, when they returned from an event, as she was changing out of her saree, Nooriya caught him looking at the faded, silvery stretch marks on her lower abdomen. Caught staring, he looked away.

'Don't you want to know how I got these, Janu?' she said. 'You never asked me about myself, before, when you didn't know me. Don't you want to know who I was, in my old life?

'All these new people, who know me today, see me as a single woman, as an interior designer, as your lover, as a Maha-Maharajji bhakt. They didn't know me in my old life, as a mother, as the wife of Ayushmann Kapoor, as I was before I came to Delhi. My parents had arranged the match, with their friend's son.' The words tumbled out. 'That's who I was, before I divorced him. In my passport, my permanent address is still recorded as my former in-laws' factory in Karnal.'

'It doesn't matter who you were, who I was, who I am. In this house, this house of love, we belong to each other, no matter what happens outside,' he responded, asking her no more questions, caressing her stretch marks. She said nothing, for now.

It was the 10th of November, the most auspicious night that year for weddings, when Nooriya got a telephone call telling her that her father and mother had died, their car ramming into a truck in a head-on collision on the way back to Karnal from a wedding in Chandigarh. Their tiny red Maruti 800 didn't stand a chance against the monstrous vehicle, which crushed it like an empty soda can. They must have died almost instantly, speculated one of her brothers, wanting to believe that they were spared pain. Someone had robbed her mother of the jewelry she was wearing, her bhabhi had said, it was nowhere to be found. Aahan's father was out of town, away at a wedding in his wife's family. She knew he wouldn't leave them and come, that appearances were too important to him, that too many uncomfortable questions and excuses would have to be dealt with.

Nooriya took the early morning Volvo to Karnal. There was no one waiting to meet her at the bus stand. She had asked her brother to receive her, but he hadn't come. Their house wasn't far away, and she carried the briefcase that Aahan's father had left behind to take his things to and fro from Sikand House, her only piece of luggage, and walked home. She walked through the low wooden gate of her father's house, rotting with many monsoons' worth of moisture.

A black-and-white sign with his name, 'D.P. Khurana, IFS (Retd)' hung on the gate. This would go now, replaced by the names of her brothers. Ayushmann, her ex-husband, was there. He had aged, and had developed a paunch, which was surprising since he would spend most of his time in the boys-only gym in the neighbourhood when they were together.

She was expecting to see him there. After all, he had been her childhood playmate and neighbour growing up, when they returned from postings abroad for holidays in Karnal. She saw her daughter, Simran, for the first time since she had been a toddler, when she had left them. She wasn't an attractive child. Simran had inherited her mother's dusky skin colour without her delicate features, taking instead, the solid, common features of her father without his comparatively lighter complexion. She wore thick glasses and had a frizzy braid, the hair on the crown valiantly resisting the taming efforts of a wide headband. She looked at her from afar, trying to gauge how she felt, when a neighbour approached her.

'Still alone, beta? What a shame. With your parents gone, under which tree will you seek shade now?' she said.

Nooriya didn't approach the child. Ayushmann looked at her, but didn't acknowledge her, or make any effort to re-introduce her daughter to her, and the duo paid their respects and quickly left. After the chautha and rasam pagri ceremony was over, her bhabhis said that there was no need for her to wait to open her mother's Godrej cupboard, that she should carry on. She returned to Delhi, distraught and alone.

That was when she decided to break up with him.

At the peak of his infatuation, she suddenly told him they had to stop. She wanted a real husband, a family of her own. Her parents were gone now and she had no one. If they carried on like this, she would never find a real relationship, a man who proudly accepted her. People were talking about them, she said. Her landlady murmured unpleasant things under her breath when they passed each other at the gate or stairwell. He had to formalize their relationship, he had to marry her, she said, or it was over, all over.

A mint-green Fiat arrived. She started driving herself to work in it, and was already gone every morning when Aahan's father drove up, hopeful. He waited outside the gate for her in the evenings. She had to come home sometime. She no longer invited him up, he had to speak to her sitting in the front passenger seat of the Fiat. How could he be hers, he implored. He couldn't break up his children's home. The farce had to continue. She didn't relent.

Months passed. Aahan's mother noticed that her husband was at home more and more, though he still slept in the guest room. They went for dinner together as a family, on her birthday, to the new Chinese restaurant at the Taj hotel. It was a lovely family outing. He slept in her bedroom that night.

Aahan's father continued to send Nooriya flowers, a standing order from the florist at Defence Colony market for twelve rajnigandhas, to be delivered to her every other day, paid at the end of the month by the company along with other orders for business acquaintances' birthdays and anniversaries. She did not acknowledge them.

He missed her. He missed watching her do surya namaskars on the grey exposed brick-and-cement terrace while he had his morning tea. He missed the easy flow of conversation, the delicious meals that she prepared for them in her tiny makeshift kitchen, and then eating them together on the coffee table – there was no space for a dining table in her house. He missed their after-dinner walks, hand-in-hand, around the dimly lit colony lanes.

She called him one day, rather unexpectedly, in the office on his direct line, in tears. Her dog, Lucca, was very sick. She believed someone had poisoned him and suspected the landlady, who was always complaining that his barking disturbed her afternoon nap. He instructed his secretary to cancel his meetings for the rest of the day and rushed over to her house. He climbed up the stairs to the barsati, his pace a bit quicker than usual. The door was partially open, and he entered to see her crying inconsolably, the large, brown-black beast lying dead on her lap. There was a pool of blood on her kurta, and a metallic smell in the air. Aahan's father kissed her on the head, and lugged the dog off the best that he could.

'He was fine – running around all day, then in one minute, he collapsed,' she said in between sobs. He went out onto the terrace of the barsati and gestured to Laxman to come up.

Laxman came up to the house and was instructed by his master to clean up the mess. Nooriya found an old, sea-green bedsheet to wrap Lucca's body in. Leaving Laxman to it, he led her into the bedroom, unbuttoned her kurta, and helped her bathe and change. He carefully sealed her blood-stained clothes in an old plastic shopping bag, they were really stinking.

Where would she bury Lucca? 'At the factory, in the garden,' he suggested. They exited the bedroom, and Laxman was standing outside, soaked in sweat, having wrapped Lucca respectably in the cloth, and placed a few of the fresh rajnigandhas, which he found in a vase, on his corpse.

Laxman and his master carried Lucca's body down the narrow staircase with difficulty, while she collected an agarbati, matches and his favourite chew toy. They stopped on the way to buy salt, and Nooriya's pet was given a decent burial in a corner of the office garden, under a mango tree.

Aahan's father drove Nooriya back himself. There was no food in the house, so she said that she would make Maggi. They had a whiskey together, both exhausted.

'Let me back in,' he said, playing with the ring on her index finger in the shape of Maha-Maharajji's hand in an open namaste.

'I want to,' she said, 'but I need something. Not like this.'

'I will leave her. I just need some time, to settle my affairs,' he replied.

'And until then? You expect me just to carry on like this, to endlessly wait. For what, I'm unsure. I left my husband, not because he was cruel, not because he was a drunk, not because he couldn't provide for me, not because he did anything very wrong. He was an okay guy. I left him because I couldn't bear the thought that the life that I lived in Karnal was all that my future held. I have grown up seeing the world, and it just wasn't enough for me. I left my child there, because I knew that she would be safe with him, that he would take care of her in a way that I couldn't. I've not given everything up, taken all those risks, all that hardship, just to be someone's mistress,' she declared. 'I need something more, not just a vague promise.'

They both sat side-by-side in helpless silence. Suddenly, she heard herself saying, 'We can both become Muslims, marry like that now, and when you settle your affairs we can marry properly, and convert back,' when the words left her lips, she wasn't sure where they came from and why she said them, it was as if Maha-Maharajji himself was speaking through her. 'I cannot be the only one taking risks here,' she affirmed with weary finality, loosening the grip of his hand on hers, and rising to pick up the near-empty bowls to rinse. 'I really appreciate your help today, I do, and I still love you, I love you very much, as a matter of fact, and want to be with you. But please help me, if you love me too, and leave, and don't come back until you have something concrete to put on the table,' she said. She was tired.

'I will come up with something, this is my promise to you,' he replied. 'Just let me stay here tonight, I don't want to leave you alone.'

'You can sleep out here, on the sofa.' She didn't want to be all alone at home tonight either. She gave him a pillow and a spare Rajasthani razai that she kept in the storage box under the coffee table, and went to her room to call it a night.

Aahan's father battled with the narrow sofa all night. When he lay down on it, it smelt strongly of dog. The pillow was wider than the seat, and kept falling off. The cushioning had sagged with time, and surrendered to his weight. The sheer curtains and ineffective air conditioner were no match for the light and heat that enveloped the room at dawn.

He felt something crawling on his cheek and woke up suddenly. It was a tick, a refugee from the dead dog's body. He went into Nooriya's cool, dark room and slid into the bed beside her, familiar yet new. He pressed against her, and kissed her eyelids to wake her.

'I'll do it,' he said. 'All I ask is that we are discreet about it, for now.'

She opened her eyes and returned his embrace. 'When?' she asked. 'Today? Tomorrow?'

'Things have to be organized, Jaan, its not like buying bread from the kirana shop. Besides, I am travelling early tomorrow morning. It's a long trip, almost two months. I'm taking my children to San Francisco, and then Yosemite, and going for a business trip to Detroit while they visit New York. I thought I had lost you, that you had made up your mind,' he replied, and kissed her on the mouth, testing the waters. 'Right after I come back, I promise.'

They both embraced Islam on his return, reciting the shahada from a scrap of paper written in English in the presence of a discreet Muslim follower of Maha-Maharajji, and took on the new names of Asif Ameen and Nooriya Ameen. Later the same day, they became man and wife for a meher of Rs 1,11,111, in the presence of two witnesses – Laxman on the groom's side and Nooriya's cousin on hers – sworn to secrecy.

She did not tell him, before the ceremony, that she was six-weeks pregnant after their unexpected reunion when Lucca died. She wanted him to commit to her, for her, not out of any pressure of a child. It was just for now, until he could sort out his affairs, then they would convert back, she reminded herself, as she signed the nikahnama.

It was to be a morganatic marriage, Asif told himself as he took the pen. He moved her into a two-bedroom apartment that he owned, which was close to the office, in one of the last respectable, gentrified neighbourhoods before the industrial area began.

SIX

LIFE BECAME COMPLICATED for Asif, giving himself to each family while he was with them like the other didn't exist. Aahan's mother did not hear about the wedding until a few months later, when a visibly pregnant Nooriya was seen around the ashram, her secret no longer hidden behind loose kurtas and dupattas; everyone knew now. Aahan's mother couldn't help it – the day she found out for sure, she was livid, and she couldn't contain herself. She barged into the guest room without knocking, where Asif was on the phone, in low tones.

'Should I call you Asif now?' she asked him tersely.

'I'll talk to you later,' he murmured into the receiver, hung up, and sighed.

'I hear that there is a woman waddling around town, she calls herself Nooriya. I believe that the man responsible for her distended belly is a man called Asif, except – that's you.

It's all quite complicated, can you explain it to me?' she said, cracking her knuckles inadvertently, a habit of hers that he hated. She wasn't supposed to do that in front of him.

'Can you stop that, please?' he said, reflexively.

'Can I stop that? Sure, when you stop making a fucking joke of me all over town,' she said, cracking her remaining knuckles inches from his eardrum. He flinched. 'I said nothing, I thought that you would stop, that you had some respect for me, for us, for this family, for your children, for the Sikand family name. Why? Why? Why would you want to humiliate us like this?' She continued in controlled hysteria now, the kids mustn't hear.

'She tricked me, darling, what was I to do?' he replied. 'I wanted to get out of it, I told her that in no uncertain terms the last time that I was with her, before we left for America. When I came back, she told me that she was pregnant, that she would come and sit outside the gates of this house until I accepted her. She's desperately in love with me, you know, and she would have done it. I've made mistakes, big mistakes, I've hurt you. I know that. I wanted to change, I had changed, but then she trapped me again.' He paused, and fell to his knees. 'You are paying for my sins, yes, but if I hadn't given her what she wanted, she would have come here, humiliated the children. Divya is yet to be married,' he continued desperately. She sat down, and picked up a piece of lint from the sofa, threw it in the dustbin.

'Who is Asif? Who says I am Asif? All my official documents are with you. Do they say I'm Asif? Who knows if it's my child? I'm trying to get out of it, I promise you. Just let's not excite her while she is pregnant, all those hormones, she will go mad and burn us all in her rage. Once the child is born, I'll settle with her, give them the Safdarjung apartment, set up a fund for them, and be rid of them. You are a good wife, a dutiful wife, being there for me when it's so difficult to,' he said, dabbing his eyes with a white handkerchief with a white S embossed on it. 'Please, I beg you, don't let our children suffer.'

A son was born to Nooriya. He had his mother's looks, and she decided to name him Aman. Asif said that it was up to her to decide the name, that he would be happy with whatever she chose. She had asked Maha-Maharajji for a name on her last visit to the Ashram before the birth, and he had written 'AMAN' on her fingertips, and drawn a peace sign on her thumb.

'What if it is a girl, Maharaj?' asked Nooriya.

He smiled. 'It won't be, but if you want a girl's name, call him Amani.' He grinned, and sent her off with a silver elaichi as prasad.

It was a difficult birth, her waters had broken three weeks early. Asif was at Sikand House that night. She was all alone. She had woken up to the uncomfortable sensation of a damp bed. At first she thought that the pressure on her bladder had caused an accident. She had read about it in Dr Spock under the dim lamplight and realized that her waters had broken, that she was in labour. She contemplated calling Asif on his home number, the one thing that he had expressly forbidden her from doing, and decided to do it – this was an emergency, it was his child she was carrying. The phone rang and rang, and rang some more, but no one answered. Sweating, afraid, she called the local taxi stand and carried her overnight suitcase, packed in advance as the literature had suggested, down the stairs and waited in the cool, dark night until a sleepy-looking Sikh driver wearing a patka pulled up and drove her to the hospital. When she was wheeled into the labour room, she requested the Malayali nurse to call her husband after 9 a.m. on the number that she gave her, the office number. She found a beaming Asif waiting in the hospital room when she was wheeled back in, giving a bottle to the infant.

He handed the baby to her with the deftness and confidence of a fourth-time father. Asif registered the infant in his birth certificate as Aman Ameen, son of Nooriya Ameen and Asif Ameen, that's who this family was, and kept the birth certificate in his safe at the office.

As long as she had the 'official' tag, the bigger house, his presence on Diwali and birthdays and anniversaries, annual family holidays, all the outward signs of legitimacy and family, Aahan's mother went along with it; it wouldn't be forever. She cut her remaining hair close to her scalp, on a whim, one morning, leaving her bald patches clearly visible. Alopecia areata, brought on by stress, the doctor had said. Patches fell off suddenly and unevenly, causing the stress that she wasn't to have. A chic wig was purchased, and she washed and coiffed it as lovingly as the hair on her own head. She gave into food and alcohol, finally abandoning her doomed efforts at dieting. She drank beer in the day and whiskey at night, ate whatever she liked without giving it a second thought, and watched old movies on the VCR. It was almost liberating not to care for herself, or for the relationship. She never, ever discussed Asif's second family with her children. They were told that their father was working late in the factory regularly and so stayed over at the other apartment. Her body and temperament both suffered, and he grew further and further away from her, initiating need-based communication on specific subjects such as the children and household. Asif developed a routine, spending most of his nights with Nooriya and some at Sikand House, in the spare room that he now permanently occupied, to keep up a façade for his children, and for society at large; he knew well the rules of the game.

Aahan's mother had never set foot in the office, aside from the annual puja on Diwali morning, with Aahan performing the main aarti with his father, closest to the deity, his sisters and mother just behind, then Laxman a respectful distance away, and finally the other factory workers. All the employees of the factory were compelled to attend, leaving their own homes and families to pray for the prosperity of the Sikands, which would presumably trickle down into their own advancement, if they weren't fired, of course.

Aahan's sisters were not encouraged to visit the factory aside from on this auspicious day either. In their mother's view, this was a place for men to have as their domain, and if women didn't interfere here, men would reciprocate and give them more leeway in the domestic arena. These boundaries were clearly demarcated in her mind, and both she and her husband had respected each other's alpha status in their respective domains. This formula, instituted since Aahan's great-grandfather sat in his shop in Dera Ismail Khan, had largely worked, ensuring peace in both places.

Nooriya saw no such demarcations. She was comfortable in an office setting, having worked most of her life. It was in the office that she had reached out to Asif for all those years, where her beloved Lucca was buried, and it was en route to this very office that their relationship had blossomed. Until Asif came into her life, Nooriya was working as an interior designer with a mid-level architect. The hours were long, the pay was meagre, and her boss was mercurial and unreasonable, capable of cruelly humiliating an employee in front of a client or co-worker. She had to kowtow to her boss's wife, for whom she became a bit of a project. She was asked to help her out with the decor and games on her children's birthday parties, answer her overbearing questions on why she was single, fob off suggestions of possible suitors, ghastly sorts, the kind which made her wonder how the matchmaker perceived her. She didn't like it one bit, but there was no option. When she decided to get divorced, her brothers had told her in no uncertain terms that there was no place for her in her parents' house. Her mother had said nothing, but sent her money for a few months, until it abruptly stopped. They were now dead. Once she got Asif, and he had started paying her rent, and eventually moved her into an apartment that he owned after the nikah, the pressure reduced and she became a freelance interior decorator. This gave her the flexibility to be available whenever Asif wanted her, and to look after the baby. She began working on the houses of the Maha-Maharajji set, further cementing her place in society.

Nooriya decided to surprise Asif in the office one day. The strain of having a one-year-old child in a small apartment was beginning to show on their relationship, and she felt that he was visiting her less and less. Everyone in the office knew who Nooriya was. A diffident watchman and smirky secretary waved her through. Asif was indeed surprised to see her, much more so when she asked him to lock the door of his cabin, lowered the shades of the window, and gave him a blowjob at his desk. If he was wavering, he was hooked again. It was this headstrong quality that attracted him to her, she was completely different from the other women he met. The excitement was revived, and she began to come to the office for lunch daily, leaving Aman at home with his ayah.

On one such day, when he was lying with his head on her lap, having fucked her and having eaten the home-cooked lunch that she had brought for him and fed him with her own hands, she took a look around his office. The fraying sofa, the Formica desk with his children's photographs under the glass, the large, garlanded picture of the Rai Bahadur, and his wedding photographs on the wall.

'It is in bad shape, Janu, it doesn't make a good impression when foreign clients come and visit.' Could she take up the task of redecorating it for her Janu?

He was helpless.

Nooriya began coming to the office every morning after that, securing for herself a tiny cubicle close to Asif's cabin. She changed the signage, ripped the flooring and had it re-laid, holding up the production floor for nearly two weeks. She redecorated Asif's office in masculine tobacco tones, removing the old chipped desk with the pictures of his children under a sheet of glass, and his wedding pictures, and replacing it with a large, imposing teak table with a bottle-green leather top with dull-gold embossing. She reframed the pictures of his parents in silver frames on the mantelpiece and added a picture of her own son, Aman, front and centre on the table, sensibly deciding against putting pictures of them together. She kept the profit she made from the inflated bills that she gave him, which he signed without looking, in a fixed deposit for a rainy day. With the redecoration complete, Nooriya kept her cubicle in the office, telling Asif that she worked better in an office environment, would he mind if she met her clients there instead of at home? – it was so much more professional, plus she could showcase the office as her work to any client who visited.

Divya, Aahan's older sister, was regularly updated about these developments by her frenemy, Akanksha, whose thinly veiled schadenfreude didn't take away from the truth of the story. Akanksha's mother, a devout follower of Maha-Maharajji, was a part of Nooriya's circuit, and so the information was deemed to be accurate. Divya repeated to her mother what she had heard, hoping to knock some sense into her, to spur her on to some action. It instead caused her to stop her single annual visit to the office, for the Laxmi puja on Diwali morning, keeping her daughters behind too, to save them the humiliation, but she continued to send Aahan.

An intelligent woman, Nooriya clocked the victory vis-à-vis the mother and daughters, but didn't pick any losing battles about the son. However late it got on Diwali night, Asif would still come and sleep in her bed, driving himself there through the smoky air, in order not to disturb Laxman on a festival. Asif discreetly and unfailingly removed any pictures of Aman before the puja day. This mutual understanding gave Asif a sense of trust in Nooriya, that she indeed understood his conundrum, and would do everything she could to make his life easier. She had to stay in his good books, this relationship had to work, no matter what. She had Aman to think of. She didn't know what she would do if he left her now. The apartment that they lived in wasn't in her name; she didn't know if it was Asif's alone or the company's asset. She would undoubtedly be thrown out of there, if something happened to him, even before the chautha, with hers and Aman's names excluded from his obituary in the paper, their existence easily erased.

Aahan's mother lived in her kaftan now, changing into a fresh one every twenty-four to thirty-six hours. She didn't bother wearing her wig at home. Divya went into her bedroom one morning, wanting to borrow a Jadau necklace for her friend's upcoming sangeet, it had to be taken out of the locker. She knocked and got no reply. She opened the door and entered the darkened room, uncomfortably chilled by the air conditioning. The room stank. An angry, booming sound emanated from the grey, blurry TV screen, the only source of light. She switched on the dim lamp next to the bed, the one with the silk crochet edging, to find her mother snoring loudly, asleep in a pool of her own vomit. A glass of diluted, unfinished whiskey was on the nightstand, and her wedding photos – 3x5 prints in sepia tones – were strewn all over the room, with some Polaroids popping out with pictures of her siblings and her, and of her honeymoon in Kashmir.

Enraged, as much at her father's actions and mother's inaction as at Nooriya's impertinence, Divya decided to confront the woman who had ruined her mother's life. She marched down to the driveway, still in her track pants and home rubber chappals, and instructed the driver to take her to the factory – sustaining her anger across the leafy city, to the barren, dusty industrial area – and stormed into the office, looking for Nooriya, knowing at the back of her mind that her father was travelling. No one dared to stop her, unsure of the protocol in such a situation. She marched into what she was told by a bemused secretary was Nooriya's office, to tell her what she thought of her, how she should leave her father alone. She had a full tirade worked out on the way over, but didn't find her. She proceeded into her father's cabin to collect herself, only to find Nooriya there, conducting a meeting. She looked bright and summery, wearing a crisp, fitted, off-white kurta, in charge of the room, holding forth on colour palates and artificial waterfalls.

The teak desk was strewn with fabric samples and architectural magazines, and she was sitting in her father's chair, with all the altered pictures. A fresh wave of anger consumed Divya, and blackened her mind to the point that she lost her vision for a few seconds. Without a single word, she walked the few steps to her father's desk, and smashed the picture of a cherubic baby Aman that had pride of place on the table for all to see. The silver frame survived the blow. Nooriya got up from Asif's chair, picked it up, and put it back.

The glass had cracked. She stared at the girl, and then her clients, aghast.

'Leave my father alone!' shouted Divya. 'Just get out of our lives! You want money? My mother will give it to you!' she continued, rather without specific authority on this point. She then picked up a glass of Campa Cola – with melted ice cubes forming a layer on the top – from the table and threw it on Nooriya's face with flourish.

The cold sticky beverage splashed all over Nooriya's face, and droplets stained her fawn-coloured dupatta. She touched her wet face. Enraged, she slapped Divya, her moist hand sliding off her right cheek, her silver bangles cold and sharp against her chin. Divya started to scream at the top of her voice, a deafening, unabating sound. Nooriya looked at her, unsure of what to do next. She was stunned at the sheer lung prowess of the young, reed-thin girl, disproportionate to her size.

She looked to the door, her clients had left, and Laxman was standing outside the cabin window, looking in. He entered, and put his arm awkwardly around the young woman, who he had held in his arms as a baby, taking her for drives around the colony in the family car.

'*Bas mere bachhe, bas mere sher, chalo-chalo, baby, ghar chalo,*' he cooed. Divya felt very tired, and crumpled onto the floor. Laxman gave her a glass of water, which she drank teary eyed, and then he escorted her to the car, all the way past the still-smirking secretaries, the front door, across the lawn in the searing heat, and to the main gate, and accompanied her home.

'I say nothing, Divya,' her mother said to her later that night, stroking her hair, 'I say nothing, because I will lose.'

After a long, restless and sleepless night, Nooriya got out of bed in the morning, dressed carefully as usual, and returned to her cabin in the factory, not before going into Asif's room and replacing the broken picture frame of Aman with two newer, more recent pictures. Asif returned a few days later, and went straight to Nooriya's place. He entered the apartment and picked up Aman in his arms. The boy began to cry, and reached out for his mother.

'Your crazy daughter came to the office and made a huge scene! Asif, I was so, so humiliated. How long do I have to put up with this? Are you ever going to leave them? What about the promises you made to me? Secure this child, he is also yours, as much as they are. All your consideration and empathy seems to be reserved for them and them alone. You have given him nothing, not even your name, yes, I have seen a copy of the birth certificate, got it pulled out from the registry,' she said.

'I will darling, I promise. Just let Divya get married. I'll talk to her,' he pleaded. He gave up, and put down a now wailing Aman, who toddled off gratefully to his mother.

The incident had left her deeply shaken, shown her what would happen if she lost. Unbeknownst to all, she took an advertisement in the newspapers, changing Aman's name from Aman Ameen to Aman Sikand, buried deep in the thousands of tiny words that reached Sikand House every morning.

Earlier, she was more willing to wait for Asif to just show up and be with her when he pleased, she now began to demand fixed days, routines, PTA attendances, to claim her share of her man. Aahan's departure for college on Aman's birthday wasn't her problem, and everyone else would just have to adjust.

SEVEN

The 1990s

Aahan would never forget that first night at university in Australia. He had reached his self-catering student flat late in the evening, tired and disoriented after a long journey from London, where he had been partying with friends studying there. London had been familiar, he had holidayed with his parents there a few times. He had had a good time, and had wished that he lived there too. When he got to his room at the university, the heating had been off, and it was pitch dark. He figured out how to switch everything on, put down his laptop bag and sighed. His flatmates, apart from one Norwegian woman, seemed to be out; she was making some salmon and steamed vegetables for her dinner, said a brisk hello, and didn't ask him if he wanted any. Completely exhausted, he trudged down to a local store that he had spotted during the taxi ride over, bought himself a ready meal, figured out how to heat it in the common kitchen, where the girl was talking to someone on the phone in another language; she didn't offer to help him. He messed up the heating instructions, leaving the basmati rice dehydrated and chewy, but ate it anyway, he was hungry and didn't have the will to unpack the tuck that had been packed for him. He went to bed, exhausted, and fell into a dreamless sleep.

It didn't take him long to accept that he didn't know how to fend for himself at all. His clothes shrank in the dryer, the food that he attempted to cook was objectively inedible. He was living off ready meals and cheese toasts every day, plus lunch in the cafeteria in between classes. His biceps and gut started to soften; he had been a committed bodybuilder once, with his mother ensuring that his daily protein requirements were met to the last gram, as per his precise instructions. By a curious logic known only to the university housing department, his three other housemates were from the Nordic countries, though one of them was of Pakistani origin. He quickly accustomed himself to their singsong norsk and standoffish, individualistic ways.

He would often go down to the university bar to have a drink, to meet up with the other desis on campus, and it was in their familiar company that he ultimately felt comfortable. He took to drinking heavily, began cutting morning classes. Those he did turn up for, he was too hungover to follow. His allowance ran out quicker than he expected, and more money was sent from home. On one such blurry night, there was a girl, another student, an Australian girl who worked at the bar after classes. He remembered dancing with her, kissing her near a trashcan behind the club. He didn't remember her saying no, not seriously anyway, he had been out of it and wasn't sure exactly what happened that night, in what sequence. All was well for a couple of days, until the campus police showed up at his apartment. The girl had complained to the disciplinary committee, mercifully not to the police, that he had assaulted her. An investigation ensued; there was grainy CCTV footage available, without any sound, of him pushing her hard, her head hitting the metal trashcan as she fell. She chose not to press charges, but the university decided that he couldn't stay there any longer, that he must go back home. He was given a week to leave, with an adverse remark on his transfer certificate. The whole affair, from start to finish, was wrapped up in two weeks.

Back home, he received a slap on the wrist from his father – a talking to over a whiskey the evening after he returned, when he was well-rested. His mother pronounced the girl who had made the accusation to be racist, frustrated and attention-hungry, and the matter was settled and never mentioned again. He got admission in the swank new management institute in Delhi, run in collaboration with an obscure college from north eastern England, where several of his school friends studied.

Of the boys, they were mostly those who couldn't afford to study abroad and didn't get admission into the acceptable colleges in Delhi University – competition was fierce there. Amongst the girls, there were the more well-off ones too, whose parents didn't want to send them away on one hand, and didn't want to subject them to the hardships of studying in the local colleges: bad food, hot classrooms and stinky bathrooms. Settling back into his old life, of late nights followed by even later mornings, cars, drivers, servants and home food, Aahan was almost relieved to be back.

While the Sikands didn't put any restrictions on Aahan, now that he was legally an adult, the story was quite different where their daughters were concerned. Whatever their personal differences were, both father and mother were preoccupied with keeping their reputations as intact as possible.

'I have different rules for my daughters and my sons, and I am very open about it, even to them,' Aahan's mother would say. 'I can't have these girls developing bad reputations, no one will marry them. The younger one is still unmarried, thankfully the older one did the right thing at the right time.'

The probability of a single girl in her early twenties breaking the rules was high, and Aahan's mother knew that. Her daughter should have started the journey of her real life: been married, soon become a mother, like she had at that age. It was when girls stayed unmarried too long, she felt, that they went astray, giving in to their natural urges. All the eligible boys of the appropriate age would be snapped up quickly, and the available pool would get smaller and smaller, with just the dregs left behind. Besides, the more time kunwari girls had in the indulgent atmosphere of their parents' houses, the less flexible they became, she felt, and had more time to mess up and ruin their chances. She wasn't going to make it easy on

Divya. She was mercurial, restless, she would lose her way, these precious years. Mrs Sikand treated her daughter like a drunk person, absolved of responsibility for a time period, to be managed, even if it was against her wishes.

She rarely left her daughter and travelled, she had nowhere to go, and no one to go with. But she had been invited to a destination wedding – to Udaipur, of the son of one of her book-club friends, who had married well, all expenses paid by the bride's family. There was to be a chartered flight, several performances and parties. It was just two nights, too tempting to pass up.

Divya had been sent to stay at her best friend Teena's house, as her mom wouldn't leave her alone with the male staff without a family member at home. Like his father, Aahan wasn't largely expected to be accountable for his time, coming and going as he pleased. Teena and Divya had grown up together, walking into nursery on the first day of school and walking out after their board exams together. Teena had her father working in Uzbekistan in some sort of mysterious import-export business. Everyone said he had another wife and family there too. Teena and Divya never discussed it, an unspoken rule between the two. This mutual understanding and lack of need to explain the nuances of their respective family situations had kept the two girls close through the years. Teena's mother was prone to taking a sleeping pill around 10 p.m., and not stirring before 8 a.m., making her house an attractive venue for the young girls to hang out.

The two girls were bored. All the people they knew were the same kids that they had known always. They had seen these boys with fuzzy moustaches, and the girls too, before they had started a lifetime of shaving and waxing and threading. They polished off the bottle of wine that they had taken from the wine cooler – it had just been gifted at a party recently and so wasn't meticulously numbered by her mother in her watertight system of accounting yet. They decided to go to The Claridges hotel and have a paan, just the two of them.

They went to the gate and got into Teena's mother's C class, a gift from her Nana. An imported car, registered in the company's name, entry level. Perfectly acceptable, but perhaps not making the statement that it was intending to. Divya, who had just gotten her learners' licence, insisted on driving. 'I could practice. You have a license, Teena,' she said. It sounded like a good idea at the time.

As Divya started the car, it bumped ahead and came to a stop. The security guard looked on nervously, he was on a double shift, covering for the regular guy, and was too tired and too disinterested to try and stop them. He opened the gate, staring into the middle distance. Divya managed to get the car out surprisingly smoothly. She breathed a sigh of relief; she hadn't exactly told Teena that she hadn't ever driven an automatic car before. In fact, she was only allowed to drive their old Maruti Esteem until she had learnt properly.

They cruised on to the main road, silent, enjoying the music and the temporary feeling of adulthood and of control. They entered Lutyens' Delhi, and took a turn at a flower-covered roundabout, decorated with the flags of India and Israel for a state visit. Divya was really enjoying the drive now, and opened the sunroof.

'Look, Teena, our playschool! Were we together at The Learning Tree?' she said, momentarily taking her eyes off the road to look at her friend. They surged ahead, and in a split second, they crashed into an auto-rickshaw. Divya panicked, and instead of pressing the brake she pressed the accelerator. There was a louder metallic screech.

'Oh shit, my mom is going to kill me!' said Teena.

The airbags deployed, further adding to their shock. They got out of the car, unhurt; that was German engineering for you, entry level or not. Though the street at this late hour was relatively empty, a few people had already gathered. The rickshaw driver was fine, but his vehicle had fallen on its side sullenly. The passenger, a middle-aged man with a blue Reebok duffle bag and bright white and new sneakers, clearly bought for the trip, who appeared to have been heading towards the railway station, was bleeding from the head, and his arm appeared to be injured too. The rickshaw driver was hurling abuses. He wanted money, compensation for the accident, both the one that just took place, and for the accident of his birth and theirs. A young man, he came dangerously close to the girls, and while gesticulating, his hand brushed against Teena's breast, possibly by accident, it was hard to say. The injured man just sat there, screaming in pain, largely ignored.

Two girls in a Mercedes and short-short outfits were too much of a draw for the crowd for anyone to give him much attention.

'Let's get back in the car and lock ourselves in, then decide what to do,' said Divya.

Teena was worried what her mother would say when she saw the car. That was all she really cared about. An only child, she had no one to call except for her mother, who was long gone for the night with the sleeping pill. Divya dialled her brother, but there was no response. Her mother wouldn't be able to help from far away, and would just get hysterical. Her father would be with that Nooriya woman, and they always kept the phone off the hook at night, given her earlier propensity to harass them through this medium, and besides she didn't even know his exact second address.

She tried Laxman Chacha's number. She knew that he was trusted by her father, and she was very fond him too, he was kind. The phone rang a few times. Divya had tears in her eyes now, the rickshaw driver was banging on the window, threatening to call the police.

Laxman Chacha answered, bleary eyed. It had taken him a moment to find his spectacles.

In fifteen minutes, Laxman Chacha was at the spot, driving his scooter, with Rajesh riding pillion. With Madamji away, he had taken the opportunity to ask his son to come stay with his parents for a few days, which was ordinarily discouraged. By this time, the rickshaw driver had managed to get his bashed up three-wheeler started again. Laxman brought cash that he had saved up for a rainy day, confident that it would be reimbursed, possibly many times over. He asked Rajesh to manage the problem while he drove the girls home. He was hesitant to do this – he didn't want his son embroiled in this mess, Sahib's problems were his, but this didn't necessarily apply in the reverse. But there was no choice, he had to protect the girls, and Rajesh was so good at handling such things .The girls crawled into the back from inside the car itself, the crowd was growing and they were too scared to get out.

The crowd wouldn't part until a settlement was reached, and the car couldn't move without risking further injury to the people surrounding it.

'*Laxman, gaadi ko aur nahin lagna chahiye*,' Teena imperiously instructed her saviour. Now that backup had come, she got her confidence back.

'*Public aa gayi hai beta, dhyan se chalna padega*,' replied Laxman.

The girls watched from the backseat of the car, behind the privacy curtains, as Rajesh negotiated with the aggrieved party. They couldn't hear what exactly was being said, but he appeared to calm things down. Rajesh paid the rickshaw driver enough to move on quietly, and even promised to take the passenger over to the local hospital. He then shooed off the waiting crowd, chalo, chalo, nothing to see here, and Laxman drove the girls home, leaving Rajesh to bring the scooter.

Completely sobered up now, Divya and Teena didn't exchange a word on the way back. It was too awkward to stay at Teena's now, she wanted to go home, and certainly did not want to be there the following morning, when her friend's mother found out what had happened. They dropped Teena at the gate, and went back to Sikand House. Back home, she thanked Laxman Chacha, shut the car door and went towards the gate. She knew that whatever she said, however much she pleaded, Laxman Chacha was certainly going to rat on her to her father. After all, he had to collect the money that he had spent on rescuing her. So there was really no point in wasting her energy sweet talking him to do otherwise. But that was another battle, for another day. For today, she was home safe. She used her key and entered the house, only to find Aahan, passed out on the floor, a small dark patch of urine on his chinos. Relieved to see that whatever she did, she couldn't be the worst behaved Sikand, even if her brother was the least accountable, she nimbly stepped over him and went to her room, removed her makeup, had an Alka-Seltzer and started watching an episode of F.R.I.E.N.D.S.

PART II

EIGHT

Delhi, 2013

Life, as Rajesh saw it, had some inescapable lotteries. An obvious one was birth and money, under the umbrella of which came a number of smaller, but significant natural advantages, like good looks and intelligence. But he had come to realize, now that he was up-and-coming in the world, that there is another significant sweepstake that wasn't necessarily tied to the other ones, and that is the place of your birth.

The urban, upwardly mobile caste system, as he saw it, had another complexion, one that wasn't tied to your actual caste but what colour your passport was. Obviously, if you were born in India, you'd rather be from Delhi or Mumbai than Hissar or Asansol. But what he wanted, in the long term, was a foreign passport in the family, for his future children. He had come a long way, and could rise higher in the political ladder, he had it in him and knew it, but he would always be a servant's son in society, unacceptable to the sahib-log as an equal. While this bothered him, he was used to it and could deal with it, but it was not what he wanted for his children. He wanted them to leave the country, to be seen as the offspring of a powerful politician, to leave the shadow of Sikand House behind completely. Being in the party, it didn't escape him, or indeed anyone else there, how India was fundamentally ungovernable, how nothing could really be done to help anyone. Primarily because more people were on the way before the existing anyones could be helped, even if there was a will on the part of the powers that be to do so. But that is another story, for another time, one with no beginning, middle or end.

This was indeed a lottery, in that it could be won by anyone, not just by the wealthy, though of course, they had an advantage here as they did with everything else. There was a legendary case of Hari Kumar, a driver in Kachroo Camp where some of his cousins lived, who had married a visiting social worker from Denmark, who was pursuing some kind of endless state-funded PhD, and had come to the camp for field work. They were wedded in the temple first, and then at her embassy. After they married, she had lived with him and his family in the camp for a while, using the communal toilet and celebrating karva chauth with the other women of the neighbourhood, until better sense and a quick pregnancy prevailed upon her to take a job at the embassy as a visa officer. Through some obscure third-world-development grant from the European Union, Hari had managed to buy a car and joined Uber. He was successful, and now owned three taxis, and lived in a two-bedroom flat in Vasant Vihar allotted to his wife, with his children – a boy and a girl – who had cold-coffee coloured skin and green eyes. They had Danish passports, of course, and attended the American Embassy School as part of his wife's salary package, now that India was a hardship posting. He hired two of his childhood friends from the camp, reliable men who wouldn't indulge in drinks or drugs or disrespect women, to drive the extra cabs. The American School moms used his Ubers to take their kids for early morning soccer practices and late-night parties, when their regular drivers wouldn't be available. They trusted him. Delhi was notoriously unsafe, and he was one of their own now, with their children playing together and the occasional school parents' social event. Freja, Farida to her new family, didn't show contempt for her in-laws, and treated them better than a local girl of a higher status would have. Bland, penniless and fatherless though she was, Freja's foreign passport had given Hari a life he couldn't have otherwise imagined, with a Danish magazine even writing an article about their love story, in full colour, with pictures of them posing at their home and at the camp. 'A moment of Hygge' was the caption on a photo of the two of them enjoying a golgappa at the local market at the camp, even though they lived in Vasant Vihar now.

Sana was studying at Arizona State University. She was an exchange student for a semester abroad at the Delhi University, at Kanti College, Rajesh's alma mater. A political science student, she came to interview Rajesh, who was a legend at the college, for a study she was doing about ex-university office bearers and whether they continued in politics (they certainly tried to) and if so how successfully (not very).

She was born in Scottsdale, Arizona, to a Hindu father and a Muslim mother, who were school sweethearts in Meerut – to the extent that this was possible, of course, in that time and place – and got married against their families' wishes. They managed to move to America, which was their shared dream. It was really all that they had in common, except for teenage lust and exploration and immaturity. The marriage ended when Sana was a year old, and she was collateral damage, deposited in Meerut to live with her Nana-Nani, with neither parent really having the time or money or inclination to look after her in America. They were very young, and still finding their way in the new world; they were determined to make it in America. Both her parents quickly remarried, but not before sole custody of Sana went to her father, her mother carelessly signing the papers without really reading them. Sana's Dadi had advised her father to do so, she ultimately didn't trust 'these Mohammedans' with her granddaughter. She didn't see her parents for six years, or their new spouses and children, until one day when she was seven years old, and playing outside her Nani's house. That was when her father appeared, with her blue American passport in his hand, and took her away, she still didn't know why. Sana could still remember screaming hysterically and trying to break free of his grip and Nani crying but not doing anything to help her, to stop him from taking her. She remembered falling asleep, still inconsolable but exhausted, on the train, and the fancy chocolates in colourful wrappers with which her father won her over.

When she got to America, she didn't speak any English and had never used a western-style toilet. The food and cutlery were unfamiliar. Until then, Nani had fed her dal-chawal every day with her own hands, dahi mixed in just right, a little meetha achaar on the side. Her father's Irish-American wife's children, her half-siblings, four-year-old twins, ate what was given to them without complaint on their own. He was again unable to look after her, and she was ultimately under the care of the old mother of her father's friend, a widowed Gujarati lady who lived in another state, whose expenses he paid in exchange, until she joined the state school (tuition free) as an in-state student. She worked on campus to support herself, and her father paid her room and board. Neither her mother nor her father had met her or spoken to her since she could remember, and she had used this grant to return to India and find her Nani, who lived at the same address in Meerut. Nana was dead now.

She came to meet Rajesh on a sunny winter morning. He was an MLA now, and had access to a small but well-located government flat close to Rashtrapati Bhawan. Naturally, he had asked his parents to move in with him. His father retained his job with the Sikands, but released the servant quarter. He continued to go to the factory, and Rajesh didn't object, or even comment. He knew that his father couldn't imagine a life without the Sikands, even if it was just as their valued servant.

He would go off on his scooter to the factory, refusing to use Rajesh's government vehicle, bursting with pride at his new status and his own humility.

On the morning that Sana came, Rajesh's parents had gone for a wedding in the village. He had cited 'official work' to get out of it, but he really just wanted to enjoy having the house to himself. She arrived in an auto-rickshaw, paid, and rang the bell. Guneeta, Rajesh's party-approved cheli, and sometimes lover, answered the door. She sized up the girl, noticing her neither-ugly-nor-pretty features, wheatish skin, large spectacles, but mostly the startling growth of dark, virgin body hair peeking out from under the sleeves of her kurti and capri pants.

She dismissed any threat from this one and immediately ushered her into the living room where Rajesh was sitting, looking intently at his phone, looking busy, really just checking Facebook. Success had improved his looks and carriage: a dentist who he had helped compromise on a dowry case had whitened and straightened his teeth, his clothes, though not expensive, were well-ironed and maintained by his mother. His Titan watch was replaced by an iWatch, a gift from a wealthy constituent. Several rings continued to adorn his fingers, given by Babajis to ward off this evil or that threat; his mother wouldn't let him remove those, or the black thread with a picture of Hanuman that he was to wear around his neck. These were non-negotiable, whatever other styles he might choose to adopt.

He went for a run every day at the park nearby. The adrenalin gave him a runner's high, and his positivity that everyone commented on, and he didn't miss that for anything. It also gave him a lean physique, though his fondness for eating a mountain of rice with dal and achaar, like he did at Sikand House when he was growing up, meant that his belly fought back, straining against his pants when he sat down.

Rajesh got up to greet her, and they settled down for a cup of sweet and under-brewed masala chai carelessly made by Guneeta. She knew that Rajesh didn't drink it anyway, just pretended to in order to make people feel more comfortable.

Sana removed the layer of malai with the edge of her spoon, sipped the tea and bit into a soggy Parle-G biscuit. She told Rajesh about her project, and about how she had been travelling around on weekends, with the money that she had saved working at Wendy's and as a night security guard at the university library. She had been to Dhaulavira to see the Harappan ruins, to the Jaipur Literature Festival where she had sat awestruck in the seventeenth row and listened to Oprah (Rajesh didn't know who she was) and was to go to Meerut, to visit her Nani. She took her questionnaire out from her jhola, bought recently at Dilli Haat but a bit frayed and discoloured already. She knew that her questions were a bit clichéd and banal, but the grant had been paid in full already, and really she just took it in order to come to India. Nevertheless, she recorded the answers:

Sana: What made you enter politics?

Rajesh: I cannot ever talk about my political journey without acknowledging Manoj Bhai, party president, who is my mentor and my guru. Manoj Bhai is an exceptional man – when he speaks, people listen. He awakened me to my special position, a servant who has grown up with sahib-log. How I must use this to help other downtrodden people. It is under his leadership that I won my election and became an MLA, Member of the Legislative Assembly, here in Delhi, last year. These are the fruits of my struggle.

I have lived two lives, one in the quarter of the kothi where I grew up, where my father worked, and indeed still works, for the same Sikand Sir. The colony was big, with large open parks, some of them with playgrounds, opposite nearly every house. I went to a local school nearby, and my father's boss, or Sahib Uncle, as I was to call him, had ensured my admission in a central school. Those are the best type of government schools, Madam, maybe not good enough for the sahib-log's children, they want private, but impossible for people like me to access without connections, without a benefactor. I was well educated, well fed, safe, cared for all my life. But this house, this life, I knew, wasn't our real place, *wahan ka nahin tha main*. My extended family, chachas, buas, tayas, lived either at the Jagdambika Camp near the railway colony, which is now part of my constituency, or in the village. My mother regularly reminded me that this is where we would end up, if my father lost his job, that I must always behave well at the kothi, there was no room for error. While my mother sat comfortably in the quarter, only helping out in the kitchen occasionally, my aunts toiled, swabbing and cleaning houses for the ladies in the railway colony near the basti, cleaning the bottoms of their children, while leaving their own offspring behind unsupervised, running wild, learning gaali-galoch, swearing and abusing. The children in the slum, they do not have these fancy prams, madam, that you see in America. They learn to crawl and walk in the galli, treading on shit from the sewer in the narrow lanes. Most kids in the area found it difficult to attend school regularly, there was no one to drop them, or they had to look after younger siblings and help with housework, while their parents were out earning money. Even if they went, they didn't understand or learn anything.

I had no such responsibilities or problems. Like I looked up to Aahan Bhaiya, Sikand Sahib's son, the kids of the camp looked up to me. Though, in the kothi, I was nobody, in my jaat, and for my extended family, I was viewed as someone who had everything: a good education, a good, clean, stable home with clean food, running water, the love of both my parents. I was half servant-child and half regular-child.

My father had done good, and I knew that I couldn't waste the opportunities before me, that I had special luck in my community, that I must make it proud, that I had to do even better. My parents – specifically my mother – never let me forget it, aisey hi line me rakha mujhe ma-baap ne. It became clear to me soon after I left the kothi, and started hostel life and college life, with the guidance of Manoj Bhai, I had to help people like me, people without opportunity, and that's why I joined politics.

Sana: Tell me about your early political journey.

Rajesh: I had started out in student politics while I was studying Hindi Honours at Kanti College. What do you think of it, Sana ji? Have you tried the bun-samosa and nimbupani made by Chaurasiya just outside gate number three? No? Go tomorrow, and tell him that I sent you. He will make it with Bisleri mineral water for you. How is the hostel these days? Accha, you are in a paying guest accommodation.

Sana ji, There were many problems on campus those days: all the students were grouped into their state and caste alliances; Jats were with Jats, Biharis with Biharis, and so on. But I grew up in Delhi, I don't belong anywhere else. And here these things are less important. The Maharashtrians can claim that Mumbai belongs to them, but here in Delhi, we are all outsiders, immigrants, with no one group having a more legitimate claim to it than the other. We want schools, water, sanitation, transportation. The rest is less relevant here. I did not believe these things to be important to Dilliwallahs. They just don't have time for this nonsense, unless someone pays the lumpen element specifically to do so.

Sana: So what you are saying is that the voters have subsumed their traditional identities to a migrant identity?

Rajesh: The younger lot, like us – they do not have the same experiences of their parents and do not carry their prejudices to the same extent. They have grown up side-by-side with people of all backgrounds, bound together by Delhi, been to their weddings, attended each other's festivals and funerals.

What was wrong is that while this is Delhi University, there are no reservations for in-state students. Madam, every university in the country has reservations for home students. I wanted a hostel room, I didn't want to, couldn't live in the staff quarter accommodation where my father worked anymore. Servants weren't allowed visitors there, so I never had a friend from school visit me at home in my life. While I was in school that was not such a problem, many of my classmates came from similar backgrounds, and were in the same situation. But in college it was different, I was mingling with people from all kinds of families. There were children of government officers, of professionals, studying with me. Then there would be a lot of ragging, and teachers and classmates, all university people, educated, padhe-likhe, looked down at a student who lived in a servant quarter.

Sahib Uncle, my father's employer, didn't really want me hanging around there anymore either, and he had promised to pay the hostel fees. I had no caste or state group backing me; I tried to get a room in the boys' hostel and was told that because I'm from Delhi I can't get the room, that priority is given to out-of-state students. Arrey? *Kamaal hai*. What is this? I have a genuine accommodation problem, but I am being discriminated against in my own state for being from my own state?

This was my plank. We demanded reservations in hostels for in-state students.

Sana: And so it was in college that you cut your political teeth?

Rajesh: The freedom that I felt in college, Madam, was like I had been reborn. I felt liberated, for the first time ever. All my life, until then, I had lived in someone else's house, with someone else's rules, eating the food they wanted to, after them, never having a choice. I had to stay in the background, unnoticed as much as possible. The pleasure that I felt in ordering from the dhaba outside college in the afternoon! Eating my lunch at the mess, at the same time as everyone!

Yes, in college there were rules and regulations, less for the boys though, you know.

He winked at her. Sana looked disapproving, but smiled, noting that his nearly six foot frame was hunched over like a giraffe trying to look inconspicuous in a hippo enclosure.

Rajesh: But my political journey, it began in a very small place, entirely by chance, in the shop of the Photostat Bhaiya on campus. The photocopy shop at college, where he still works, is the meeting ground for all the college politicos. I didn't know that when I befriended him. I used to go to his shop, like everyone else, to get notes Xeroxed. He ran a side business of recycled notes of the best students, the toppers, in the college for every course through the years, and sold them in packages by their names: 'Kabir Chemistry Honours Notes', or 'Shobhini English Honours Notes', and so on. They were spiral-bound and everything. People would buy these near the end of the year and mug them up to write exams, the course hadn't changed for years.

I was regularly visiting his shop, and offered him advice about how to keep the dying money plant on his desk alive. He did as I said, and he felt such joy when it came to life and went on to thrive. We struck up an equation on gardening, which I have always loved. Soon, his little kiosk had green baskets hanging outside, made him happy. He knew about my money problems. I had a job at Mc Donald's to meet my expenses, but money was always short. He offered me another job, delivering the notes that students bought to their rooms, collecting the money and bringing it to him. I became his runner, and like this, delivering notes, I got to know many students on campus.

Sana: Oh! I had two jobs on campus last year too.

Rajesh smiled.

Rajesh: Then you know how hard it is to manage everything. Photostat Bhaiya really liked me, he was of my biradiri too, you see. Even today we have family relations, my picture is hanging framed on the wall in his shop, you go see. He got me some other work too, one that made me who I am today. His cousin is my political mentor, Manoj Bhai. He told him that I was a boy to watch out for. Manoj Bhai, who was also in his early days of struggle, put me on a task: handing out leaflets for the party, which was in its nascent days, at the campus for the upcoming election. There was to be no pay, but I did it. I positioned myself near Photostat Bhaiya's shop, and was damn annoyed, Sanaji, when people looked through me, walked by. So, I started distributing free sachets of sugar and ketchup with the leaflets, which I got from my shift at McDonald's. These single-serve items were in high demand amongst the hostel people, perfect condiments that they were for the tea and Maggi that was constantly cooking on the sly in the rooms.

Manoj Bhai heard about all this and was very, very impressed. He called me to meet him, and took me under his care. From that day to this, madam, I was and am his follower.

I remained in the university for over five years, and did an MA in Hindi to stay on. Three years, of which the first year is spent settling down and grappling with a new life, just isn't enough to get the best out of campus life. At first, you are ragged, made to do inane things like dancing to some bawdy song and give a rose to a girl, and it gets more menacing for those who don't cooperate. Once they accept you, you find your feet. If you want to be active in politics you are initially given mundane jobs like putting up posters and distributing pamphlets; a year and a half, or half your time there, has passed before you get a serious chance. Then, by the time you get any actual influence, its time to leave, to look for the job that you are probably never going to get. Aside from studies, I had to pass, at the very least, which I did thanks to Priyanka Hindi Honours notes from Bhaiya's shop, from year to year, and I was working part time at the McDonalds on top of everything, as I told you, near the college to earn money, so my time was even more limited. The job was yet another ehsan, a favour, from Sahib Uncle, his college friend was the franchisee.

Whatever work Manoj Bhai gave me, I did. When he said step aside, let so-and-so take centre stage, I did. After a lot of hard work and struggle I was elected university joint secretary, in my third year of college. You see, madam, in those days, I was fresh from Sikand House, I did not have the confidence for neta-giri, to make speeches in front of everyone. I messed up badly in one speech, and Manoj Bhai told me to take more of an organizational role after that.

He realized that he had said too much at that point.

Rajesh: On my suggestion, my party started a campaign for students originating from Delhi in the college to band together. Manoj Bhai is very open to the ideas of younger party members; this is his strength. Our demand was 25 per cent reservation for in-state students in the hostel. It was under this plank that I always worked. I feel that it is important to have a clear purpose and message, however small, if you want success. The campaign was noticed, and soon all the students in my college knew my name, and not just because I was couriering the notes! Manoj Bhai even gave me a pager, so that I could stay in touch. Many other, bigger political parties have been in touch with me over the years, but I wasn't interested in this jaat-paat, you understand, Madam? Divisive parties. And besides, there is nothing in politics for me without Manoj Bhai's hand on my head. Not then, not now.

Looking back, it was a blur, but was the busiest, happiest time of my life. Life is both short and long, isn't it, Sana ji? There were many hurdles; uncooperative hostel wardens, seniors who thought that they could hold me back with their petty games, frustrated, underpaid teachers who misused their time-bound powers in a student's life to make my life hell, like they do to all students, really. Not to mention my own situation at the time. But from where I stand today, I can only see the good in the past. If I hadn't been born in Sikand House, no matter that it was as a servant's child, I wouldn't be where I am today. Aside from the fact that I got a good education, good clothes and food, I learnt to deal with a number of different types of people. Young children, unless they are unfortunately put to work early, only interact with their family members, who are likely to show them the good side of human nature and not the bad – I had seen all kinds of behaviour though my life, from the madam-log to the baby-log to the other staff – so, I had a head start, and perhaps was much better equipped to deal with the politics around the campus than other students from better backgrounds.

He felt that he was rambling now, and decided to stop.

> Sana: Did you feel your education helped you? What do you think about so many uneducated and corrupt people being in Indian politics?
>
> Rajesh: What a silly question, Madam, obviously my education helped me and, of course, it is not ideal that there are uneducated people in politics, but until more of us are educated this is inevitable. What kind of question is that?

Rajesh grinned. He was bored and wanted to be amused. He sized up the girl sitting before him, adolescent body, too-big spectacles, not pretty but certainly not ugly. 'So, tell me, Sana ji, about you. Your parents. Whole family in America?'

'I was born there,' was what Sana could get herself to say.

Rajesh suggested that they continue the interview on a visit to his constituency. 'You must see the real India, Sana ji. Consider it a part of understanding my political journey, of understanding your subject. Just give me a few minutes and we can leave. We can continue the interview en route.'

Rajesh summoned his official driver, and went inside to asked Guneeta to 'do the needful' at Jagdambika Camp. Guneeta scowled. She didn't like where this was going. 'Arrey don't saro,' he said to her. 'Have you seen this girl? Just look at the hair on her legs. Not my type at all, yaar, just trying to increase my profile. Maybe her interview will be carried out in a foreign paper. I need you to wait here please, I am expecting some papers, Mummy-Papa are away, who will receive them?' He pressed against her and bit her lower lip slowly, the way that he knew she liked, and set off with Sana, who had been outside, taking pictures with a complicated-looking camera, of some neighbourhood stray dogs basking lazily in the late winter sun while she waited.

NINE

SANA AND RAJESH got into the rear seat of the sarkari Innova allotted to Rajesh. She looked at the party stickers, both half-peeled and new, stuck carelessly yet cheerfully on the windshield, with writing in Hindi, a language she spoke but could not read. He asked her to pick up some leaflets and an empty can of Coke to make space, which she did. Sana noticed his perfectly manicured hands, animated as he spoke, and wondered about his contrasting attitudes to vehicular upkeep and personal grooming. As they drove past the Gauri Shankar Mandir (she thought it was Ram-Sita but he corrected her), past a spanking-new Starbucks and a local clubhouse preparing for a wedding that evening, they continued the interview.

'You were asking about how my education helped me, Sana ji. If I had to distil down to one word what my education did for me – English. It was that I could speak English properly.

It is a gift, given by circumstances, to a selected few in this country, which can open up so many doors. I first learnt English growing up at Sikand House, from talking to Aahan Bhaiya, my employer's son, watching cartoons and movies, and reading his old books, Hardy Boys and Enid Blytons. I went on an official tour of the United Kingdom recently, a delegation to study council estates as a model for urban housing. It was my first trip abroad, Sana ji. My parents were so excited, they insisted on dropping me to the airport and everything. When I got there, I expressed a desire to my hosts to try scones and clotted cream – I had grown up reading about these foods, and had no idea what they tasted like until six months ago!

'The only thing of use that I learnt in school and through Aahan Bhaiya's books was English. Still, I was not so good, even at Kanti College. Hindi was okay to get by over there. Later, when I left college, I had to get a job, quickly. Politician's ke beta-beti can join politics full-time in their early twenties because they don't have to earn rozi-roti. I had to earn, to find a place to live after college life finished and I had to vacate the hostel room. Returning to my father wasn't possible. And I wanted to continue in politics also. Here also Manoj Bhai helped me. He helped me get a job at a call centre in Gurgaon. They gave me training. It was a night shift, graveyard shift as it is called, and I would work at the time set by you Americans. Worked for me. Gave me an income, and I shared a rented room, my room partner worked in the day and me at night, and it left me free for my political work too. And my parents used to visit me there, so proudly. We celebrated festivals there, freely, the way we liked to. My parents experienced the freedom that I had, since college days, for the first time with me. What busy days, Sana ji. *Pata nahin kaise kiya sab kuch.*

'At the call centre, my English became perfect. I can confidently speak to a reporter like you,' he said with an American twang. Sana didn't correct him, she was a researcher and not a reporter, and she had never heard an actual American speak with that accent. 'The party can use these skills, my knowledge of the ways of bade-log, unka uthna-baithna kaise hota hai, ladies se kaise baat karte hain. My party has dedicated people, very hard-working, but they haven't had the privileged upbringing that I have had, so I have a special place.'

A teenaged beggar girl with a listless newborn in her arms started tapping at the window of the car with a metallic ring, worn to make more noise against the glass, to attract more attention to her fate from those who tried to look away.

Sana pulled out her camera, rolled down the window, and started taking pictures of the girl. She was in a colourful lehenga with pretty glass bangles. Emboldened, the girl stroked Sana's hair, asked for money from her 'pretty didi'. A kinnar saw an opportunity and left her post at the adjoining three-wheeler.

She approached Sana's window. '100 rupees for a picture! *Jodi salamat rahe!*' she proclaimed.

Rajesh's driver got out of the car, and shuffled the duo along. '*Chalo, chalo, sarkari gaadi hai*,' he said, pointing to the stickers.

The baby, of indeterminate gender, was still asleep, as if it had been drugged. Rajesh leaned over to Sana's side and rolled the power windows back up. 'These are people, Madam, humans. Not animals in a safari park to photograph,' he said roughly, as the traffic light changed and the car moved along. Tears rolled down Sana's cheeks. Taken aback, Rajesh pulled out the hanky that he always kept in his pocket and handed it to her, and put his hand on hers to comfort her. He noticed that her forearm had some words written on them, with a blue ball-point pen, partially hidden under the rolled-up sleeves of her loose flannel shirt. 'We are all' and 'Light' was all that he could decipher.

'What's this?' he asked. Sana rolled up her sleeve and showed him the entire quote.

'We are all broken, that's how the light gets in,' it read.

'I look up motivational words and phrases, on the internet, and write the ones that appeal to my frame of mind on my arm every day. It helps set intent, gives me positivity. My healing master, who I met while working in Montana, taught me,' she explained.

'I can see in your eyes great loss, great pain, great sadness yet a lot of strength. Something bad has happened to you, and you have come out on the other side,' Rajesh said.

She was happy, here, in this car, talking to him, and she told him the highlights of her life story: her parents great love that didn't last, their determination to stay in America at all costs, those lonely days with her father's new family, her Nana's death, of which she learnt years later. 'I want to go to Meerut, to ask Nani why she sent me away like that, all those years ago. Was it planned? Or did he just land up one day without any warning?' She had never received a satisfactory answer from her father.

Rajesh listened intently, and as they entered a by-lane that led to the camp, she noticed that his hand had lightly brushed against hers a few times again, but she didn't mind.

Guneeta had phoned Chotu, Rajesh's cousin and unofficial coordinator of his visits to the camp (he was hoping for a more concrete role soon), to organize everything. A foreign mem was coming with Rajesh Bhai to the camp, he had to show her slum life, the brighter side. This would include four-or-five women in ghunghat, tilak and garlands, ringing the bell at the Shiva Mandir behind the market, as the welcome party, before they began the grand tour. They would end with some tea, biscuits and Bisleri, at the charpai near the tea shop. He was seriously thinking of turning the routine into a slum tour that he could ticket if he was able to find some connection with foreign tour operators. He went into the houses of a few aunties watching television in their nighties and cutting vegetables, and told them to change into sarees, bring their puja thalis and come to the mandir. Five hundred rupees was the rate decided upon, rather inflated with a cut for Chotu built in, as there was little advance warning.

The ladies and Chotu assembled at the Shiva Mandir. It wasn't too hot yet, but the sun was threatening them with what was to come in the months ahead. Regardless, the gallis of the basti were always in shade, staying cooler until longer, but cloying in the humidity of the monsoon months. They saw the Innova pull up around the bend of the garbage dump, and sprang into action. They covered their heads – saris in parrot green, fuchsia, and magenta – and started to sing a welcome song, tunelessly, as the only nightingale in the group had recently found part-time employment in the colony nearby and wasn't available at such short notice. As Rajesh got out of the car, he dived down to touch the feet of Phulwati Tai, the oldest woman there. They first applied a tika on his forehead, and then on Sana's. Phulwati Tai took Sana into a sweaty, comforting bear hug, dislodging her glasses with her jovial enthusiasm.

Sana had, in all her years in America, craved this kind of spontaneous affection in a non-sexual situation. She had rarely been alone when she was in Meerut as a child. She slept in a double bed, with the jet-engine like sound of the cooler and the smell of its khus, between her Nana and Nani, reaching out to feel Nani's earrings in her sleep to check that she was still there, until the day her father took her away. When she got to America, it was just so quiet outside. Her father and stepmother were too exhausted by the twins and work and each other to attend to anything beyond her very basic needs. The elderly lady who had fostered her later was efficient, Sana was clothed and fed and sheltered adequately, yet in a way that felt distant and clinical, as if the woman did not want her getting attached.

She couldn't quite tell what she had been missing all those years. Not until that moment. Touch without expectation. Memories of her grandmother and Meerut flooded back and she returned the hug with more enthusiasm than it was given. Rajesh noticed, and gave her a kind, intimate smile.

'This is where my family is really from, Sana ji. Come, have a look,' he said, lightly placing his hand on her back to guide her through the crowded galli. The settlement that Sana visited, like so many others, was on railway land, encroached upon slowly and surely, with this political patronage or that. Ultimately, each resident was a vote, or a future vote where the wee ones were concerned, and no one wanted to mess with it. On the contrary, over the years, signs of permanence could be seen and heard through the landscape. Pet dogs, the hardy local mongrels. TVs with their satellite antennae, coolers, motorcycles, discarded chips packets and chocolate wrappers. Electricity wasn't a problem – it was easily diverted from the local transformer. What caused the most strife was water, and the lives of the residents revolved around it – its procurement, storage, distribution, management, and even removal as it bred dreaded mosquitoes. The settlement was a small city with better addresses and worse ones, and Rajesh had instructed that Sana be shown just the gentrified parts, where the factory workers lived, with their relative education and grooming.

Nevertheless, Sana's American eyes hadn't seen anything like it. She had hazy memories of Meerut, a child's unreliable flashbacks, and that too mostly of her Nani's house. She knew, theoretically, about poverty, bad living conditions, slums and so on, but to be unexpectedly confronted with them on an afternoon on which she had originally planned to do a quick interview and then proceed to Dilli Haat for momos, blindsided her. She could barely contain her shock at the lives of others, cooking, cleaning, grooming, fighting, continuing their rather uncomfortable existence so unselfconsciously, and possibly even happily, under the ever-watchful gaze of their neighbours. The worst that she had ever seen in the US, in terms of living conditions, was pure luxury compared to this.

At the end of the afternoon, Sana sat with the ladies at the charpai at the tea shop, and sipped some masala chai in a thick, small glass. Biscuits and namkeen were served on steel plates with shared spoons. Sana was hungry, she took a spoonful into her mouth, closing her lips around the warm steel, causing the ladies to giggle. '*Kya kar rahi ho, jhoota ho jayega!*' they scolded.

Rajesh sat with the men around a plastic table at another tea shop a short distance away, but Sana was still aware of his presence every minute. Tea and gup-shup done, he sauntered over to the ladies' area and asked her if she was ready to leave. She gathered her things and they boarded the Innova, with Chotu and Phulwati Tai seeing them off, and the rest of the crowd following deferentially a few steps behind.

Back in the car, and keen to extend the outing, Rajesh suggested that they stop at the new Radisson hotel that had recently opened nearby so that she could use the bathroom. It was impossible for someone like her to do so at the camp, he said. They alighted at the lobby, and the large bearded doorman, seeing the official vehicle but not recognizing Rajesh, saluted smartly.

While she was away in the restroom, Rajesh sauntered over to the coffee shop in the lobby area and took a seat. She returned and he asked her if she would like anything.

She ordered a beer, along with a greasy club sandwich. The contrast between the camp and the hotel, the sweet tea and sharp beer, as well as the awareness of Rajesh's presence had both exhausted and energized Sana.

She had never felt so absorbed, so immersed by anything or anyone as what she saw today. She had often sought the company of women, they were kinder and gentler than the members of the opposite sex. She was ashamed to admit to her American friends that she was still technically a virgin.

Rajesh trained his eyes on her, attentive and watchful. He liked what he saw in her – a sweet girl, a kind soul, so grateful and overwhelmed by his attention. A quick decision maker, Rajesh's ability to read situations and people had always given him the edge where his education and circumstances had failed him. He wasn't one to waste time on a long courtship, getting to know someone. His parents were proud and overwhelmed with the offers they were getting for him, on par with the going dowry rate of an IAS officer. Still, he would not get to see those girls for too long either, and the pressure was building up to get things moving. His mother wanted company and help and grandchildren now. But this sweet girl and her blue passport could offer him something that couldn't be easily monetized – undying grateful adoration and a ticket out of the mess, should the whole show go up in flames.

Rajesh insisted on dropping Sana back to the apartment in Lajpat Nagar, where she was staying as a paying guest. She told him that the other girls had told her never to be dropped back by a man, as the landlady would sit in the balcony in the evening and observe the girls returning, and call her names if a man dropped her home. She suggested that Rajesh get dropped first, then he could have his car drop her. Rajesh agreed and texted Guneeta to check on her whereabouts – she had left, the papers were on the dining table and the key was under the ficus gamla at the entrance.

En route Sana told Rajesh more about her family: leaving her Nani, suffering from nightmares, and how she had travelled all around India, in a bus as she was short of funds, but had avoided trying to meet her grandmother yet; she just wasn't ready. During a particularly sad part of the story, he reached out and held her hand, and didn't let go until the car pulled up at South Avenue, lightly massaging her palm with his fingers. She said that she had left her scarf behind; he invited her in.

As they entered the dark foyer, he fumbled with the keys: his mother, for all his success, could not wrap her head around keeping full-time domestic help. '*Koi help nahin chahiye hame, no help ji, mujhe paise de dena*,' she had said to him with unarguable finality.

Inside, Sana asked for a glass of water. She followed him into the kitchen as he poured it from a scratched, yellowing plastic bottle in the fridge. 'I still have one final question to ask you,' she said. 'What is that X-factor, in your opinion, that got you where you are today, when so many others have failed?'

'Good luck,' he replied simply.

She set the steel tumbler down on the kitchen counter, and noticed a small cockroach scurry away into a crevice behind the tiles. Rajesh took her in his arms and gently kissed her, tenuously nibbling on her lower lip. She responded gratefully; she was beginning to wonder if she had misread his signals. The words tumbled out before she realized it.

'I'm a virgin, and I'd like to give myself to you.'

He stopped and looked at her, taken by surprise. He didn't imagine for a moment that American girls of her age could be virgins. 'I was attacked once, in high school, by a senior, while walking back to Aunty's house. He was violent and I managed to get away, but was never interested after that, until now.'

'We shall marry tomorrow. Then you will be mine,' he declared. He had decided. Better to get the job done before his parents returned, then after some drama his mother would accept it. He was the de-facto head of the family now, after all. He had already been more intimate with her than all the girls regularly paraded before him by his family, overdressed and desperate.

Sana had wanted a shepherd all her life; all these years of making her own decisions had existentially exhausted her. She nodded meekly and smiled. She was ready.

Back in the Innova, he held her hand on the ride back to her paying-guest house, and instructed her to be ready with all her things by the morning; he would be back for her.

He dropped her a safe distance away, and as he drove back home, he was satisfied with his choice. Once he had taken a decision, it wasn't in his nature to dwell on how he could have done it differently, and the possible setbacks and problems ahead. He just went with it. He knew that the best way to sort this out would be swiftly, and then the onus would be on Mummy ji, and on Guneeta, to accept it. He resolved to help fix Guneeta's marriage with some up-and-coming party cadre, to settle her in some way, and put her out of his mind. Back home, he slept soundly and woke up early as he was used to doing, and began to organize everything. He called a party man, a pandit at a small temple in R.K. Puram, telling him that he wanted to organize a quick wedding, without telling him for whom. The priest asked him to come later that afternoon. A photographer was called, ostensibly for a bhumi pujan. He set out of the house in the morning, wearing the kurta-pyjama and Jawahar jacket that he had for his swearing-in ceremony, stopping on the way at the Ritu Kumar store on Ring Road that he had passed a thousand times, with pretty salwar kameezes in the window. Inside, the sales lady looked at him with contempt and curiosity. Clearly a lower-class type whose stars had changed, she assessed, and approached him with a bright smile

'Can I help you? *Aapki help kar sakti hoon, sir?*'

He had seen that look before, and replied, 'I need a wedding outfit for a woman. In red.' He used his American call-centre accent, confusing her earlier judgement.

'NRI?' she thought to herself, unconvinced, as she led him into the bridal section at a corner of the store. It was all exorbitantly expensive, laughably so. He wandered through the shop, and selected a scarlet sharara-style set from what the sales girl called the pret collection.

'It's not handwork sir. Machine-made, viscose,' she had said reproachfully. He paid, satisfied with his choice, and headed off for Lajpat Nagar, a few minutes behind schedule.

He found Sana waiting outside unquestioningly, a slightly battered suitcase by her side.

He looked for signs of relief on her face that he had indeed arrived, but there weren't any. She seemed not to have fathomed the possibility that he wouldn't show up.

He smiled at her, disarmed by her trust, and handed her the shopping bag with the outfit. She could change at the priest's house. As they pulled up at the temple, behind the DDA market, she asked him about his parents, what they would say.

'It won't be easy,' he replied. 'My mother will hate you for a year or two, but ultimately she will adjust. I suggest that you embrace this hatred as a stage of love, without reacting negatively, and it will pass earlier than you think.' That was all that there was time to say, as he saw a flower seller outside and realized that he had forgotten the garland for the jaimala ceremony. Sana, no stranger to hostile domestic situations, said nothing, and looked out of the window.

Inside the temple, he took Sana across Hanuman ji's mandir – reminding her to remove her keds outside – to the pandit's office at the back.

'This is the bride,' he said. Panditji looked at her. Sana never wore makeup, which made her look younger than she really was. The pandit was concerned that she might be underage, and he asked to see some identification. Much as Rajesh's star was on the rise, he couldn't risk a police case. She fumbled in her jhola and took out her passport. Rajesh too peered at it, realizing what a fool he was to not have checked it himself. All was in order.

'And where is the groom, Rajesh Bhaiya?' asked Panditji.

'That would be me,' replied Rajesh.

At the mandap, Sana appeared in the sharara, accompanied by the priest's wife, who had been persuaded to help her get ready once it became known who the groom was. Normally, she didn't like to be disturbed from her daytime soaps and knitting for 'this kind of drama'.

Rajesh looked at Sana and couldn't help but smile – the panditayan had convinced her to apply some bright red lipstick, the only one that she owned, saying that it would look good in the pictures. She was swimming in the clothes that he bought her, both lengthwise and breadthwise. Her body was obviously more supple and unripe than he had imagined it to be under her clothes. He was imagining sucking at her little breasts later that day, but the panditaiyan broke his fantasy with a shrill, '*Kaisi lag rahi hai dulhan, Bhaiya?*'

And just like that, it was over. In forty-five minutes, give or take, they were man and wife. It was a blur, seven rounds of the fire, jaimala, a few pictures on his driver's phone (the photographer never showed up), and all was done. Sana realized that she was wearing sneakers when she had gotten there, but had no choice but to wear them with her ill-fitting wedding outfit, as the priest's wife had already stuffed her clothes into a small plastic bag with 'Big Bazaar' written on it and sent it to the car, keeping the Ritu Kumar bag for her own use. They then headed back to Rajesh's, to their home, stopping on the way at the Defence Colony Sagar for a late lunch – they were both ravenous and there was unlikely to be any food in the house.

As they got home, he found Guneeta sitting on the steps outside the house. He sighed. News had clearly travelled faster than that Sagar idli. She appeared to have been weeping, her face streaked with kohl. He hoped that there wouldn't be too much of a scene. He opened the door and the two women entered with him. He said to Guneeta, with Sana still holding her bags, 'I am your brother now, and this is your Bhabhi. I expect that you will give her the due respect of the wife of your party MLA.'

Guneeta was furious, she hurled herself at Rajesh and started hitting and kissing him at the same time. Sana left the room and went into the kitchen, the only other part of the house she had seen, and drank a glass of water. She waited there, and went inside the shell that she had created so successfully for herself. She was naïve in some ways, but not in others, and she knew that Rajesh had to have been with other women. She could hear the raised sounds of Guneeta's voice and the placating one of Rajesh's. She peered through the door to see that she had ripped open her kurta and a dirty white bra was barely concealing her large breasts. He bent down, gently closed whichever button hadn't broken, and whispered something inaudibly in her ear. Then they rocked back and forth together for a while, before she got up and started walking towards the door. Sana slipped back into the kitchen, pretending to have been there the whole time. Rajesh entered a few minutes later, and held Sana in his arms. She smelt marigolds and Charlie on him, probably Guneeta's perfume, and sweat, mixed in with what must have been an early morning cigarette.

'I'm sorry that you had to see that on the very first day of your married life,' he murmured, but offered little by way of explanation.

He held her hand and showed her the house that was now her home. She had already seen the living room and the kitchen. Additionally, there were two bedrooms with a shared bathroom. One was Mummy ji's and Papa ji's, with blue tube lights and the walls filled with large religious posters. There appeared to be no favourites – on the contrary, care seemed to be taken to ensure that no god in the Hindu pantheon was offended by exclusion. The only other decoration in the room was a panchang calendar, and an enlarged picture of Rajesh being sworn in as an MLA. Then, finally, he took her to his bedroom, their bedroom now, sparsely decorated, with bare walls, and a profusion of plants on the windowsill and courtyard outside, and told her to make it up her way. Then, he asked her to take off her clothes while he watched. The commotion with Guneeta had delayed things long enough; he had to have her now.

Later, at dusk, while she was getting settled in, he went to the living room, dark and cold except for a single tube light on the wall, and called his mother. She answered on the fourth ring, just as he was contemplating hanging up. There were joyous sounds in the background, of a dhol and singing, sounds of a wedding house.

'*Mummy ji, maine shaadi kar li hai*,' he said.

Two days, a bus ride, a train ride, and a car ride later, Babita was back. She had a lot of time to think on the journey and unlike Guneeta, she had time to work through the gamut of emotions before she met her new daughter-in-law. She raged and cried and threatened and fumed the entire way back to her husband, who sensibly said nothing. But, being a practical woman, as the train was approaching Ghaziabad, on the outskirts of Delhi, her face changed and she adopted a determined expression.

At the train station, the driver was waiting, but not Rajesh and her new daughter-in-law. She clocked this snub. Back home, she rang the doorbell and Rajesh opened the door. She saw him and, as if on cue, copious tears started streaming down her face. She sat down, and in a stage-like manner, her daughter-in-law, Sana, appeared from the kitchen, wearing a long, loose red sharara, the same one that she was wearing in a framed picture of the two of them on the side table. Rajesh had instructed her in advance to touch his parents' feet, which she did, clumsily, tripping on the chunni of the outfit, but quickly regaining her balance.

Babita said to the new couple, 'You have done what you had to. We have to accept it, your didn't give us a choice. Now you must promise, Sana, to always look after me and always have a place for us in this house.'

Sana served them the penne arrabiata, a salad and brownies that she had made. She was never much of a cook – she ate to sustain life rather than to evoke pleasure. They enjoyed the pasta and brownies, but couldn't wrap their head around the leafy, oily, slippery salad.

The following year, Rajesh's son, Aditya, was born and his American passport arrived shortly thereafter. A party was thrown, forty days after his birth, at the community centre nearby. Much to Sana's horror, Babita had blackened the baby's eyes with kajal, to ward off the evil eye. Rajesh thought he looked terrible, like a servant's child. Sahib-log never did this kind of thing. He protested, only to be met with an affectionate yet firm 'tu chup kar!' from his elated mother.

Sana, whose childlike body had returned to its original state already, wore her red wedding outfit once again. She got her son a slender Turkish evil eye charm from Dilli Haat and put it on his tiny wrist, mother-in-law and daughter-in-law united in their desire to ward off the evil eye from their new-found good fortune.

Rajesh's son had indeed proven lucky for him, and his party was now in power in the state – in a coalition, but still. The event had to be correctly managed. There were, on one hand, people from the basti, his father's colleagues from the factory, who he wanted to, and had to, invite. On the other, there were important party colleagues, people who could help him get ahead, who wouldn't necessarily want to mingle with the former because of the many pleas, requests, sifarish, chamchaagiri.

It was warm but not hot, and the venue, the neighbourhood community centre, had a big garden and an indoor space. A solution was found – the VIP guests would be entertained in a separate airconditioned area inside the venue, and the others would remain outside, in the gardens, with huge fans spewing mist to keep the guests cool. Chotu would be the gatekeeper, and allow only the right people into the sanctum. Babita appointed herself to the task of chaperoning Sana and the baby, who were to sit in a separate, adjoining room, and, of course, collecting the sagan envelopes, which she kept safely in a large black leatherette purse, her only handbag. Laxman was to attend to the factory employees, and the Sikands, if they came.

Aahan was the only Sikand who made it. Sweating profusely, he entered along with his driver, who went his own way thereafter, to join his appointed tribe at the event. Laxman dropped everything to look after him. Without bothering to greet the factory workers – he had limited patience with that sort of thing, and it was a friday night after all, he had to get on with it – he went straight inside and handed Babita a sagan packet, which she weighed to guess its contents. He briefly sized up Rajesh's not-unattractive wife, whom he was seeing for the first time. She was soothing the wailing infant, who looked like a panda, so he didn't talk to her. But he wasn't done yet. He needed to meet some of Rajesh's political friends. There were labour problems at the factory, and he needed help. He sat on the sofa, sipping an awful orange soft drink in a thick highball glass that was forced into his hand by Babita, wondering all the while if his white blood cells would be able to ward off its attack. Laxman hovered around him, internally anxious for the man-child to leave so that he could get on with enjoying the event as a proud grandfather and not a servant. He stood beside him, because he couldn't get himself to sit in his presence, and Aahan didn't suggest it.

Aahan was contemplating whether to ask Rajesh to make the introductions, or to abandon the idea – every moment of this event was torturous for him.

Suddenly, there was a flurry of activity. Manoj Bhai, the party president himself, had arrived with his wife to bless the child. There was frenzy amongst the crowd outside, he was immensely popular, a revered figure. He moved without security, and stopped regularly to greet people, many of whom he knew personally and greeted by name, as Rajesh led the couple slowly inside the sanctum. The swelling mass of people couldn't be contained anymore, Chotu just wasn't enough.

'*Kundi lagao, lock lagana padega darwaze pe*,' Aahan heard Laxman tell Chotu. Aahan had had quite enough, and pushed his way through the crowd of people, calling his driver to end his party too, and to bring the car. He left with his task of the evening unfinished, and no one noticed him go, not even Laxman Chacha.

TEN

IN ALL HER years, until now, Sana had been a rolling stone, gathering no moss. She had drifted from place to place, fully immersing herself in whatever situation she might find herself, but her circumstances had wired her brain to remain unattached, no matter how engaged she outwardly appeared to be. She made what seemed to be deep bonds with people she met over the years, in school and college and in her summer jobs, only to go dark on them once she left. She didn't operate any social media accounts.

When she married Rajesh, she quickly brushed up on her Hindi, watching daily soaps with her mother-in-law, and learnt to cook Indian food from YouTube videos, quickly realizing that her mother-in-law wasn't a much better cook than her, always having eaten the food made for the staff by the cook employed for this purpose at Sikand House. Having lived in America most of her life, she was already attuned to most domestic chores, and didn't think any household job to be beneath her, much to Babita's delight. She bought a dishwasher, and repeatedly but patiently explained to her mother-in-law that she must rinse the plates before loading them. Rajesh's mother considered this to be double the effort and defiantly continued to wash her own plate by hand. She bought a washing machine and loaded the entire family's clothes together, segregated in whites and coloureds. Babita said that she was intimidated by all the buttons, unlettered as she was, and this task was off her hands now, though she still insisted on ironing all of Rajesh's clothes herself.

Sana also upped her husband's acceptability with the sarkari neighbours, some of whom looked up to her because of her foreignness, her American twang, and her broken Hindi spoken with a foreign accent. Other, more well-to-do ones saw her as an equal because of it, overlooking her new family's lower class roots and ways. She began to be invited to their kitties and pujas, her advice was taken on US college applications for their children. She wasn't sure how, but she began to be introduced as being from New York, a place she had never visited. She didn't bother correcting anyone after a while, Arizona seemed just too remote to relate to in the present, and anyhow, she was from nowhere, and belonged to no one – before now. The birth of her son tied her irreversibly to Rajesh.

Some of the women were devout followers of a Guru called Maha-Maharajji, and she went to his ashram with them occasionally. She had gone through a phase of spirituality, like many college students, and it was heightened by her personal situation. She had learned the art of Reiki and pranic healing while working at a wellness resort in Montana one summer, and tried to communicate with her Nana through a Ouija Board.

When she first went to Maha-Maharajji's ashram, she didn't get an audience with him. She was told in hushed tones by the ladies with whom she went, her neighbours out in one of their husbands' government-allotted vehicles for the day, that the first day that Maha-Maharajji gives you an audience outside of the group pravachans – which were irregular since they took place only when Maha-Maharajji was taken over by the holy spirit – is the day you are blessed. It could be a week after you started seva, or a month, or never. That was how he tested the purity of his devotees. He didn't care for position and status, they said. It seemed to her that the ashram was creating an artificial demand to make them value their experience more, but she went along with it, to humour them. They were her new friends now, after all.

'Go with it,' she wrote on her arm, the third time that her new friends invited her for an ashram outing.

Maha-Maharajji had, many years ago, receded into his gufa, his quarters. The place lay deep within the compound and was heavily patrolled and guarded. Years ago, when the numbers at the ashram began to swell uncontrollably, some of the original devotees had decided to form an Ashram Management Committee, the AMC as it began to be known, to look into its finances and administration. Lakhs of rupees came in as donations every month in the early days, with the figure rumoured to touch the crores now. Access to Maha-

Maharajji had to be managed, the exposure to throngs of people was interfering with his meditation, diluting his divine energy. Additionally, there were rumours of sabotage, of people who were trying to harm him, threats to his life.

This was not a democratic setup by any stretch of the imagination. Maha-Maharajji had nominated all the members in the early days, when the committee was formed, and they soon began to hold the positions in perpetuity, releasing just a couple of spaces every year, for 'special invitees', ostensibly to give new disciples hope of advancement, but in practice to fast-track anyone useful. Many new measures were brought about by the AMC, the latest being an issuance of smart cards and a special fast-track access gate to registered devotees. Convenient as it was for devotees, it helped the AMC keep track of who was regular and who wasn't.

The AMC had its eyes and ears all over the compound, and combined with the attendance data, they decided who met Maha-Maharajji and when. This gave them immense power in that realm, and requests came in every day for a quick audience, from powerful people, rich businessmen, politicians and bureaucrats.

Nooriya had kept up with the Maha-Maharajji set, and was a life member of the AMC. It was getting difficult now to manage. Asif was hankering to move permanently to Shimla, he said he was done with Delhi, dusty and superficial as it was, and it held no attraction for him now that his children were grown. Aahan could run the factory, and his daughters were both married, settled. Aman was in Mumbai now too, Nooriya had added. If she was going to live away from Delhi, she would have liked to have a new member nominated as a special invitee to the AMC, who was loyal and grateful to her, her eyes and ears, who would protect her interests during the transition.

Nooriya, and indeed the AMC, had registered the presence of the group of MLAs wives who had started visiting the ashram regularly. It was their job to do so, to keep track of whoever might be useful to Maha-Maharajji, to the trust, to the cause, of course, and to keep them coming back, especially since the Maharaj himself wasn't in the best of health anymore. Some of the women had an audience with him, and others hadn't. They wouldn't be kept waiting long, just long enough that they valued the experience. Nooriya was sifting through their profiles, which had been shifted higher up in a heap of applications to have a darshan, something everyone was made to fill out when they got their smart cards. She figured out who Sana was as soon as she saw her application.

While she knew about most of the characters who inhabited Sikand House, she hadn't actually interacted with any of them, except for the unfortunate incident with Divya, and the one time all those years ago that she briefly spoke to her mother, and sighting Aahan at the office from time to time, on the rare occasions that she still went there, and having to sidestep him like a thief.

Curious, she asked for Sana to be handpicked from the crowd the next time she came, and brought for an audience with Maha-Maharajji, sans her companions, via her office, of course.

Sana was efficiently flagged on her next visit to the ashram. She entered the compound, took off her shoes to give to the sevadaar, trying to ignore the sensation of the hot, gritty floor on the soles of her feet. He asked her to go to the AMC office, which was known to be the gateway to meet Maha-Maharajji. Her companions swooned and chattered excitedly, but quickly realized that none of them had been chosen. Sana did as she was told, and wordlessly followed another sevadaar, who wore a badge around his neck on a long red strap that read 'On AMC Duty', glancing back to give her companions an apologetic smile.

Nooriya was waiting for her at the office. She gave no indication that she knew anything about Sana, and warmly greeted her with an open-palm namaste.

'Maha-Maharajji can tell a soul with a clear heart the minute that he or she enters the compound,' she said. 'He is omnipresent within the ashram. But let your meeting with him be yours alone, do not share it with anyone else. Like no one has specifically spoken about their darshan with you, you mustn't with anyone either, for it will colour their own perception of the saint with yours, taint their darshan.'

Sana now understood why she hadn't actually heard an account of what it was like to meet Maha-Maharajji from anyone, and before she could process the information, a form was brought, putting into writing what she had just agreed to, and she was made to sign it. The consequence of breaking this promise to the AMC was being banned for life from the ashram. Sana went along with it, and was shepherded on by Nooriya to another, smaller anteroom.

The room was in pure white Makrana stone, and had mirrored walls. There were no lights, but a number of white candles reflected infinitely into the mirrors. A single wooden chair and matching low table were the only pieces of furniture, and brass bowls with water to wash one's hands and feet were appropriately placed. Nooriya told her that she would be back, and asked her to prepare herself to meet the Maharaj. Alone in the room, she looked at her reflection and attempted to fix her dishevelled hair with her fingers. She dipped her feet in the water, and found it to be ice cold. A towel hadn't been left to dry off with, so she used her chunni the best that she could. Soon Nooriya returned, and guided her into the next room, which opened through a mirrored panel revealed to be a hidden door.

The contrast of the next room attacked the senses. There were red walls, a red-and-gold throne with red velvet upholstery, red carpets, and a cloud of incense. Religious music played on a boom box, in a language she didn't understand. On a red-and-gold four-poster bed in the corner of the room, she saw The Master, wearing a red satin half-sleeved pyjama suit, and a number of rings and necklaces, propped up by an orthopaedic pillow of some kind, which unfortunately didn't conform to the red theme. Nooriya urged her to move closer. She inched ahead, still overwhelmed by the sudden change in her surroundings. As she got closer, she saw that there were mirrors strategically placed all around his person, on the walls, the tables, the ceiling, which surrounded her on all sides with reflections of his image juxtaposed in red. The Maharaj's eyes appeared glazed, almost as if he were unconscious, and his face was flushed scarlet, matching his surroundings. His breathing was shallow, and she thought she spotted some needle marks on the veins on his forearms.

Sana wondered if he was present within his body at all. Nooriya went close to him, and shouted in his ear at a volume that startled her, but barely got a response from him. 'Please bless this disciple, your new daughter, Maha-Maharajji!' she said.

He stirred a little, and drooled from the left side of his mouth. He managed to hold up his hand in an open palm namaste and stroked her head, possibly inadvertently.

'Maha-Maharajji has been meditating and fasting for days now, he is very tired,' said Nooriya, as she guided her back into the white room and then out into the office, the real world. 'Maha-Maharajji needs the services of people like you, Sana, educated, loving, free souls. Please do give some time to volunteer at the AMC, I will guide you personally,' she added. She gave her a visiting card with her mobile number scrawled on it, and took hers in return. She once again reminded Sana not to speak of the details of her meeting with Maha-Maharajji with anyone, as she ushered her back into the crowd, to her waiting companions – they had come together in one car and couldn't leave her behind.

Nooriya invented a role for Sana, as an 'overseas-Indian devotees liaison officer'. She drew the young woman into it, reminding her that it was more glamorous than the first tasks of most sevadaars, who were to act as shoe keepers and the canteen servers. Sana began to work closely with Nooriya to define what her designation actually meant, spending hours every day in her little office with her, brainstorming and assisting her with her work, learning the ropes. As much as Sana had tried to make a go of spending time with her mother-in-law during Rajesh's long absences, she relished the attention and companionship of Nooriya – an educated, older woman with a purpose, who was offering her a life beyond cooking and cleaning and watching TV soaps with implausible plot twists.

Sana was quick to finish her share of the household tasks, and began going to the ashram nearly every day, in the late morning, leaving her son, bathed and fed, in Babita's care. She would eat lunch there, usually with Nooriya, who brought enough for the both of them, returning at dusk to help prepare dinner for her husband and father-in-law. Nooriya bought her five delicate mulmul salwar-kameez sets and a pair of pretty juttis as a gift, suggesting that her old jeans-and-T-shirt-with-sneakers look didn't suit her current status. She invited her to watch a play with her at the Kamani auditorium after they finished with work one day, and took her for dinner to the Habitat Centre after.

Rajesh didn't take up her long absences with Sana, despite his mother badgering him regularly to do so.

'That Nooriya madam isn't a good influence on her, she is a home breaker. Don't let her manhoos shadow fall on our family,' Babita admonished, enjoying the sound of her own cautionary words.

Rajesh ignored her. '*Rehne do Mummy, tumhe kya problem hai, apna kaam kar ke jaati hai na? Nooriya Madam ko hamse kya lena-dena? Kaam nahin sambhala jata to rakh lo ek maid!*' he said firmly. He believed that a woman like Sana, an educated woman, couldn't be locked up with Babita all day, and even procured a Wagon R from the stable of cars of someone who owed him one so that she could drive herself back and forth, much to his mother's chagrin. Sana seemed focused and motivated, and he was happy with the change he saw in her. He was further pleased when he learnt that she had managed to organize darshans with her Baba ji for his colleagues' wives – profuse thanks came his way when he ran into them. Babita was not one to give up without a fight, she firmly believed that the girl must not go 'out of hand', that she was young and pliable and must learn to put family first. '*Foreigner hai, uski ma bhi nahin hai, kya seekha hoga, kuch paise bhi nahin milte wahan se*,' she would rant to herself, murmuring under her breath while doing her chores – chores that she wanted her daughter-in-law to take over.

Babita began to grumble about being the sole caregiver to her grandson. He ran everywhere now, and put everything into his mouth, she was an old woman, she couldn't chase him around, and couldn't be held responsible if he hurt himself. She began to get mysterious backaches just when Sana was leaving the house, and would profess an inability to look after the child all day, insisting that she herself needed looking after now, if her daughter-in-law had the time.

Sana started taking Aditya, her son, to the ashram with her every day, attaching a second-hand rear facing car seat that she bought at an embassy sale to the back of her Wagon R, much to the amusement of her husband and in-laws. Watching him in the ashram was difficult while concentrating on her work, which she very much enjoyed. He was too big for a body carrier and too small to walk around independently for too long, and the ashram premises weren't stroller-friendly. She couldn't bear the idea of a nanny trailing them everywhere.

'I wish there were good daycare here,' she said, exasperated by the child who just couldn't sit still, to Nooriya. 'There isn't even a changing table at the ashram. It's so difficult to look after him here,' she continued. An idea came to her as she spoke. She wanted to pitch starting a crèche on the premises, with teacher–bhakts presiding as sevadaars. She made a proposal on an excel sheet, late at night, while Rajesh was out politicking, and presented it to the AMC. While Nooriya was inclined to encourage Sana anyway, it was objectively a fabulous idea. A part of the ashram trust's vast resources were used to develop a state-of-the-art facility, overseen by Sana and Nooriya. Babita had unintentionally cemented her daughter-in-law's position in ashram politics, and she was soon made a special invitee on the AMC, with Rajesh, Babita and Laxman getting a special audience with Maha-Maharajji to commemorate the occasion, on a day that he was mercifully more lucid.

Rajesh was happy that Sana had found purpose, that she had managed to climb up the trust's ladder so quickly – it could be useful. Nooriya, whom he, his mother and father called Nooriya Madam, but Sana, with her American ways and without the baggage of servitude, called Nooriya, invited them to have tea with her at the AMC office after they met the Maharaj. Rajesh quickly accepted on his and Sana's behalf, but said that his parents had to go, to take the baby home.

Laxman understood, and, miraculously, so did Babita. They went home in Rajesh's official car, firmly rejecting Sana's suggestion that she undo the car seat from her vehicle and give it to them, leaving Rajesh to return home with Sana in the Wagon R.

At the AMC office, tea, nan khatai and chiwda had been organized, and Nooriya introduced Rajesh to the other AMC members. A young, rising star in the government, and indeed in the new order of things, and his foreign-born wife, a special invitee at the AMC. Their transformation was complete.

They left the ashram at dusk. Sana gave him the keys, assuming that he would drive. 'You drive, I have many calls to make,' he replied, hastily getting into the passenger seat. They decided to stop at Evergreen Sweet House on the way home for a quick bite, and some time alone. It was there, over mineral-water golgappas, that he told her that the only time he had access to a car was when he became an MLA, and hadn't the opportunity to learn before that. The official car came with a driver, and he didn't want to humiliate himself by trying to learn with him by his side, instead said that he was simply too busy catching up with phone calls in the car to ever drive.

ELEVEN

AFTER HE MARRIED Sana, Guneeta didn't let Rajesh forget about him. She would call him incessantly, and he had to leave his phone face-down on the dining table to avoid his mother's questions, but it would nevertheless continue to vibrate demandingly.

'*Kiske itne phone aate hain, raat-din beta, bada admi hai, lekin khaana to kha le*,' she admonished. He blocked her number. She began to call Sana's number instead, playing 'Hit Me Baby One More Time' by Britney Spears on full volume when she answered.

The morning of Sana's birthday, Rajesh awoke early, and went to the living room to read the newspaper, to find Guneeta sitting there, with a large balloon bouquet in the colours of the American flag behind her.

'*Pagal, yahan kya kar rahi hai? Kaise ghusi andar?*' he exclaimed.

'*Chabi abhi bhi matke ke neeche hai*,' she said playfully.

Laxman entered the living room in his kurta-pyjama and saw Guneeta.

'*Aise hi wish karne aayi thi, Papa, bas ja hi rahi hai*,' he said to his father, and hustled Guneeta to the door. He agreed to meet her again the next day – it was on this promise that she left.

They met the next morning, at a multiplex cinema, at a show of an animated movie, which wasn't likely to be crowded.

'What do you want from me, Guneeta?' he said exasperatedly. 'It's over. I'm married. I have a child. My wife is pregnant again. Stop harassing her.'

Guneeta examined her long talon-like nails in the dim light of the screen, freshly gel painted in rainbow colours at a kiosk at the mall while she had waited for Rajesh to arrive. 'You can't get rid of me so easily. After all, I am a member of this party that has given you everything. Just a few soft words and I'll go away? No, no, no. Just … no.' She wagged her index finger, which had a little diamond embedded in the polish. She was really enjoying her nails. 'I don't think so. *Aise thodi hota hain*,' she declared.

'I'll think of something, just stop calling her, please,' implored Rajesh. He ate some popcorn from the bucket wedged into her seat, brushed his greasy fingers off, got up and left.

'*Picture to dekh lo, paise kharche hain*,' Guneeta said to his retreating figure.

He called her later that week. 'I've managed to get you a job at Manoj Bhai's office. High-profile job hain, one of a pool of four secretaries who sit outside his room, teen ladkiyan aur hain. They work in shifts, two at a time. He works all hours. You have to field his calls, get him his tea, take notes, keep him happy. I'll be needing you, keep in mind, *mujhe batate rehna kya hota hai wahan. Tu ek kaam kariyo, CV bhej de, Guneeta, formality to banti hain*,' he concluded.

Working at the party president's office in any capacity was a significant career move for any party worker. The PP was not computer literate, and would call the secretaries in, one at a time, leaving the other to handle the phones, and dictate notes to them at a furious pace, which they would transcribe in shorthand. The first time he called Guneeta in to his office, alone, she was unable to keep pace with his words, and kept asking him to go slow.

'Don't you know any shorthand?' He was visibly irritated.

'*Abhi seekhi hain, job milne pe, Rajesh ne bheja mujhe*,' she replied, leaning over the desk.

'Accha? So what use will you be to me until you learn properly? *Jao, phone uthao, doosri ladki ko bhejo*,' he said, dismissively.

She went over to his side of the desk. '*Sir, ek chance toh do*,' she said. '*Stress khatam kar doongi.*'

More experienced now, she managed her expectations, knew what she was getting into. She knew that this would end, like it had with Rajesh, and she had to maximize her time with him, to get something, she wouldn't get another chance after this.

On her way home from work one day, she bought a small camera shaped like a pen from a shop in Palika Bazaar, where her neighbour's son worked. He guided her on which one to buy. The next time he called her in for dictation, she left the pen casually amongst the mess of leaflets and garlands on his table.

Guneeta got in touch with Rajesh, and asked him to meet her. She wanted to share what was happening in PP's office with him. Rajesh met her at a Café Coffee Day, in an office complex, empty on the weekend.

He heard her out, and said, 'Do you have no shame at all, Guneeta? *Kuch bhi sharam hain tujhme?* I sent you there to work, *yeh sab karne ke liye nahin. Abhi to kaam shuru ki hai tu*. Manoj Bhai is a good man, he isn't like that, *kyun party ko barbaad karna chahti hain? Ek yehi raasta hain aage badhne ka tere pas? Bade aadmi se chipakna, phir ussey blackmail karna?*'

Guneeta looked at Rajesh and sipped her cold coffee. '*Tujhe kya pata*, what do you know of the things people have to do to get ahead in life? *Kuch pata bhi hain?* You have always gotten everything easy. *Acchey ghar me raha, school-college padha, maa-baap ne sab kuch kiya tere liye, tu kya jaane struggle kya hoti hai?* What it is to live in this world without your parents' protection? Party president ke liye English jhadta hai, officers ke samne, that's why he has kept you. But everyone knows that you are a slime, *kaam to tu teda hi karta hai, na*.' She drained her glass and put it down on the table.

'I am also educated, BSc degree ki hai, online MBA *kar rahin hoon, lekin kisi ko kuch farak nahin padta. Jo teri strengths hai*, you use them. I'm just doing the same. Mujhe kaun just like that hi promote karega? Did you? Dropped me overnight, American ke liye. You are only talking to me because I'm harassing you, I know that. Aur waise bhi, did I force him, *maine kaunsi uski izzat looti hai, tere party president ki, ki tu mujhpe toot pada?* Why didn't he refuse? He was in the position of power, not me. Rajesh Kumar, what's good for you isn't necessarily good for me, and I am here to help myself. Don't lecture me, help *karega ki nahin, bata de*,' she said.

Guneeta showed him the three grainy videos that she had recorded. Getting involved in this was risky, he thought. But the PP had a lot to lose – his beloved family-man image, and indeed his entire public image – in case Guneeta decided to go down that path, that is, to self-destruct in order to take him down. Rajesh had known Manoj Bhai for many years, and watching him in different situations, he understood the PP's psychology. He had a wife, two children and a watchful, widowed mother – he had a good-boy complex, a need to be viewed positively by others, which was almost debilitating. Rajesh texted him, asking to meet; the PP gave everyone his mobile number in an effort to be more approachable.

A meeting was granted soon after. His was an organized sort of operation, they liked to be on top of things. Guneeta was on shift that day, but she was to take a sick day, and was not to accompany him for the conversation. She wouldn't keep a cool head, Rajesh felt, after hearing her tirade at the coffee shop, and, after all, no man likes to be exposed as an adulterer, to be pushed into a corner, with no opportunity to emerge with his dignity intact.

When he got there, it was prime time, 6 p.m., and the place was buzzing. Constituents, MLAs, hangers on, all looking for the boss's time and attention. Endless cups of oversweet chai and weak coffee were being served from the Nescafe machine, with intermingling, hybrid tastes. Getting a moment alone seemed impossible. He waited, used this time to network, catch up on the khabar, the gup-shup. Time passed; more important people were attended to, several bouquets of gladioli and roses were accepted and tossed aside, boxes of mithai were distributed. Finally, his turn came, and he felt the spy pen that Guneeta had given him, checked once again that he had put it in his front pocket, and got up nervously.

'*Aaja aaja, Rajesh beta!*' called the PP, as he entered the office, decorated with Rexine sofas, a boss chair with a faded, striped towel draped on top, and brightly lit with blue tube lights. The boss was in no mood to listen, jubilant and energized with the affection and sycophancy of the people, with his power, and he continued to hold court with the people still in the room. No matter, Rajesh continued to wait patiently. It was close to 9 p.m. when the PP prepared to leave, stopping to ask Rajesh: '*Vaise, tumhe kaam kya tha, beta? Aise he milne aa gaye?* Good, good ...'

Rajesh said nothing, instead pulled out his smartphone, and showed him one of the pictures that Guneeta had forwarded to him, one of the less explicit ones, to make his point with minimum embarrassment. He had his attention. The PPs demeanour changed in an instant, and a dark cloud came over his persona. He asked for the room to be cleared, and Rajesh had his complete attention now.

'*Aaj tak maine koi galat kaam nahin kiya*. You sent this girl, *tune bheja ussey, phasane ke liye mujhe*? After all that I have done for you? *Saale, servant quarter me reh raha tha, maine*

MLA banaya, aur kya chahiye tujhe?' he said to Rajesh, in a rage.

'To help you, sir. To make this go away,' replied a slightly trembling Rajesh.

Arrangements were made to settle Guneeta. A not-insubstantial sum was paid, via an ambitious constituent, and a new job at a multi-national corporation was organized. Pictures were deleted, though Rajesh retained a copy of them on a pen drive for good measure. The party president replaced his entire pool of secretaries with four middle-aged Malayali men hired from an agency.

Rajesh had been secretly deeply disappointed at not getting a ministerial berth when his party had joined the flailing government. He was still young, Manoj Bhai had told him, and he had to wait his turn. He had no choice, no power, and had to accept it. He knew that he wouldn't be perceived as fresh blood for long, he had seen many a pathetic 'youth' leader, desperately clinging to the tag as the years passed by, only to be replaced, forgotten. He sealed the pen drive in an envelope, wrapped it in duct tape, and gave it to Babita to keep safe. That evidence was his opportunity, his leverage, when the time came, waiting in his mother's cupboard.

All he had to do now was wait for the right moment, to hope that it came at the right time. 'Timing is everything' was one of the phrases that Sana regularly wrote on her arm in the mornings. One of his colleagues was bound to trip up, and he would call in a favour, he would replace them. They were an uneducated, inexperienced, ragtag bunch. The others in the party, with the exception of the party president and a few select others, came from backgrounds just like his, but mostly without his advantages and exposure.

Later that year, several party MLAs, and some ministers, went to a trendy nightclub in Hauz Khas Village, where a petty rubber manufacturer was hosting a birthday party for one of them, a young man, just forty-two. The bar was the kind of place that, had the wheels of fate and time not favoured them, they would ordinarily be working at as waiters and bouncers and cooks.

'Rights of admission reserved' was written with people of much higher social status than them in mind – they wouldn't have even been contenders to enter as guests. Not yet used to the privilege, the open bar with flowing booze, the gumption to stare at the high-class teenage girls in short skirts with the same rights as the sahib-log, many of his colleagues got dead drunk. Rajesh watched, sipping on a Sprite, and left early. Subsequently, there was widespread misbehaviour – the best of it when the sports minister, a former gym trainer, punched the bartender for telling him that the bar was closed, and the worst of it was reported to be when one drunken MLA openly began masturbating on the strobe-lit dance floor. Videos were taken, and all the TV channels picked it up, blurring out the nasty bits, of course. The verdict was divided; while there was public outrage, many young men in the slums privately took pride in how their own had stormed the sahib-log's bastion. That notwithstanding, action had to be taken, and, more importantly, it had to be seen to be taken. Suspensions, expulsions and a reshuffle later, with his son, mother, father and a heavily pregnant Sana watching, Rajesh was sworn in as the minister for Labour and Social Welfare, a ministry that he had specially requested the PP to assign to him.

The ministry was tenuous, and indeed, their entire government was too, a fragile coalition. Unlike his earlier days, when everything was a bonus, and anything ahead looked better than what had gone by, Rajesh now had a lot to lose. He had Sana and the children to think about.

'They know nothing about living like servants, they wouldn't be able to survive like that, they shouldn't have to. I won't let them,' he would repeat to himself through the day like a mantra, distracting him from his daily duties. He realized when Chotu pointed it out to him, asked him what he was saying, that he was unconsciously murmuring it out loud unintelligibly one day.

Rajesh was nervous, waking up to the crying of the new, colicky baby at night, and unable to go back to sleep. He would pace the dark, quiet living room, thinking of what lay ahead. Should the government fall, and it was likely that it wouldn't complete its term, Rajesh would have to vacate the government flat.

And then what? Sana didn't have a penny to her name, or any real monetizable skills. They would have nowhere to live. Where renting a house was concerned, politicians were the most disadvantaged group in the country, followed closely by lawyers. Landlords would routinely refuse to rent their premises if they suspected even a tenuous political connection. They feared, quite legitimately, that such tenants were powerful squatters and would use their political connections and legal acumen to intimidate and harass them and would not vacate the property when asked to. This applied to the high-command and foot soldiers of the party equally, cutting across ideologies and party lines. Along with a determination to promote their kin, however undeserving, this was a unifying problem faced by the political tribe. Party lines were often crossed just to get that elusive government accommodation, no matter what other ostensible ideological or moral reasons were professed.

'What must it feel like, to live in a house that someone has just given to you, for nothing, from where no one can ask you to leave? Where you belong?' he would wonder, when he could worry no more. With Rajesh's background working as an added disadvantage, he was almost certain that no one would rent their property to him. He couldn't imagine that his parents, so full of pride now, would be welcome again at Sikand House – their room was occupied by someone else – nor did he wish that fate upon them.

Sikand Sahib, who was his father's benefactor all those years, had taken up residence in the Shimla house with Nooriya Madam years ago, retiring from Delhi life. Rajesh had heard that his younger, illegitimate son, Aman, was very good-looking and trying to make it as an actor in Mumbai. Sahib Uncle had left the house and factory for Aahan, and his daughters were finally married. He was free. Aahan wasn't going to show any benevolence to his parents. The stakes were high and he needed a house of his own, at the mercy of no government or election or employer, where no one could throw them out.

TWELVE

Asif had worked hard for years to ensure that the factory pretty much ran itself. It had taken decades, but with the right people in key positions, it was finally happening. There were loans, of course, but which successful business didn't have some liabilities? He decided it was finally time to take a back seat, to spend more time in Shimla. The double life had taken its toll on him, and he was exhausted. The girls were settled now, and he hoped that with the guidance of professional management, Aahan would, going forward, be able to manage things on his own. Over the years, he had siphoned off enough to live a comfortable life in Shimla for the rest of his years; he didn't need anything more. The rest was for the next generation, for Aahan.

There was never any question that the factory and the house would go to Aahan, and not to Aman. His younger son was an effeminate boy, he had dreams of making it in the entertainment industry, and Asif had set him up in a two bedroom-hall-kitchen in Andheri with a monthly stipend to start him off. Asif was sure that he was gay, and put it down to his mother's over-coddling. Nooriya accepted neither theory, and went into a huff if either were so much as alluded to. Asif decided it would be better if Aman stayed in Mumbai, more peaceful for everyone, most of all for the boy himself. He didn't judge, really, but he didn't want all that his father had set up with such difficulty after the Partition to go down the drain. He was merely its custodian, after all, and believed it should go to his eldest son, his legitimate one, and to his grandson after that.

Aahan finally got the chairman's cabin, vacated by his father. Free from his father's shadow for the first time, Aahan tried to be a model boss. He woke up early and hit the gym at 7 a.m., finding a different, more focused crowd and energy there in the morning, which included professionals and service people, rather than the businessmen, landlords, housewives and wannabe housewives – women on the lookout for a husband – who got the 11 a.m. slot that he usually preferred. Showering and breakfasting at the gym, he was at work by 9.30 a.m.

He kept this routine up for months, despite his fondness for Oban at night, and for 11 p.m. dinners after that. Unfortunately, one day, not long into it, he woke up and realized that he didn't give a shit about how shock absorbers were made and sold, that he had nothing to add to the process, and lost his mojo. There was no one to stop him; his father was preoccupied with his apple orchard in Shimla, and nobody bothered to tell him what was happening. Aahan was in charge now, after all, with no one above him. He began reaching the office closer to lunchtime, and leaving at 4 p.m. to avoid the traffic.

On a particularly heavy Diwali, huge losses were made at the cards table. Aahan's judgement was clouded by the aforementioned Oban, and he brushed aside Parul's gentle pleading that he leave the table – it was a party, after all, and she couldn't seem too concerned. The debts mounted: the latest BMW, holidays in the Maldives with his children's friends and their parents. Apparently no one hired maids for their children anymore, only professional nurses would do. Jewelry for Parul, the diamonds that she had always wanted.

At work, he dismissed the threat of Chinese competition poaching one of their biggest buyers, and he brushed aside the exit of the CEO, a driven man who had lost interest in the business when the boss had, and had taken a job in Doha, for the much better salary and lifestyle.

Aahan continued in his way, money was still being made. Production dropped a bit, and he adjusted targets accordingly. The workers' union was getting stronger, and Laxman saw it. But he was just an employee, and felt it out of place to say anything. They started demanding a longer, structured lunch break, overtime after eight hours, and paid sick leave, even for non-permanent employees. Black bands and symbolic strikes, only of a couple of hours at a time, began. In an unrelated incident, a couple of workers got into a fight on the shop floor, apparently about a woman and an unpaid debt. There were injuries and demands for compensation on all ends. Aahan didn't refuse or accept their demands. Lethargy and inaction, rather than a lack of sympathy for their cause, was why he sat on the problem for a while. Plus, there was a fortieth birthday to attend in Prague, followed by a boys' trip to Budapest, minus Parul, that he was looking forward to immensely. It was going to be sick, he had heard amazing things about Eastern Europe. He would deal with it when he returned. The workers could cool their hot heads in the meantime, and he would come in when tempers were less flared.

His trip lived up to his expectations, if not his budget, and on his return, he needed a couple of days to recover. There had been a medical incident, an irregular heartbeat, undoubtedly precipitated by the substances he had consumed whilst travelling. Mercifully, nothing had happened on the flight and whilst he was abroad, it was so much easier to manage things in India.

He returned to the factory after over two weeks. There were nearly a hundred workers, in their blue uniforms, waiting at the gate. He was in his monstrous SUV, a company car, imported just a couple of months ago. He asked the driver to slow down, to see what was happening. Unbeknownst to him, it was the driver himself who had notified the union about his exact time of arrival. He professed ignorance and drove past slowly, trying not to hit anyone. The crowd tapped on the car windows and peered in. An overenthusiastic participant in the protest digressed from the script, improvised, and broke the wiper of Aahan's beloved vehicle. Aahan lost his temper, stormed out of the car and slapped him. All hell broke loose.

Someone from the crowd smashed the window of Aahan's car defiantly. A barricade had been set up, with old tyres, and the now frenzied mob set fire to it. Laxman was neutral in the protest so far, but seeing Aahan Baba in danger triggered a Pavlovian loyalty to his master, and he somehow managed to shield him and take him to safety, riding pillion at the back of his scooter. People respected Laxman very much, of course, but now his son was an important man too, and no one dared to stop him.

Back home and safe, Aahan felt a crippling physical version of fear for the first time in his life. His entire body was shaking as he hugged Laxman and thanked him with a genuineness and intensity that surprised them both. He went to his room, locked the door and poured himself a drink. He began to cry for the first time that he could remember since before he was a teenager. Things were going very wrong, at a speed and force greater than he was able to control. He needed his father's help, he needed it now. He would have to go to Shimla, to that woman's lair, to seek it.

Aahan decided to fly to Chandigarh and drive to the mountain house from there. He hadn't announced himself, not knowing with any certainty how welcome he would be in Nooriya's domain. While he was confident that his father wouldn't turn him away, he couldn't be so sure that he wouldn't make an excuse to stop him from coming in the first place. The flight to Chandigarh was smooth enough, but the long, bumpy drive from the airport to the house got him on edge. Nearly four hours were spent in interminable traffic on the road, with ugly, ill-mannered tourists piled into buses streaked with vomit, jamming everything, stopping for selfies and dropping chips and biscuit packets everywhere, followed by feral monkeys looking for leftovers.

As he arrived at the house, the old chowkidar, a toothless, ancient pahari man, recognized him immediately from his younger days, and waved him through. He got out of the car, and Lucy, the resident bhotia, jumped on him, squealing and barking in recognition of an old friend.

His father was in the garden facing the house, wearing a jogging suit, loafers and hat, clipping his rose bushes. He looked up, smiled and hugged Aahan, almost as if he were expecting him. It was evening now, and the journey had been long. They chitchatted in the garden until dusk, about the children, the orchards, the simian problem in Shimla. Neither one mentioned Nooriya, though Aahan scanned the premises from time to time for signs of her, expecting her to show up at any moment. When he returned from a shower, ready to have a drink with his father, he concluded that she wasn't around, and breathed a sigh of relief.

They dined together, but Aahan couldn't keep up the pretence of having come solely for his father's company, and his father knew that there had to be more to it.

He recounted to Asif all the recent events at the factory, neglecting to mention his absence, delay and fear. Asif listened carefully. Once he was done, there was silence for a while, aside from the clinking of ice in their glasses when they took an occasional sip.

'So what do you want from me?' asked Asif.

'To come back. To fix it,' he replied.

Another long silence. He would have to think about it. Could he mull over it until the morning? It feels later here than it is, up in the mountains. He must go to bed. Aahan was taken aback at his nonchalance, but said nothing. The older man went to his bedroom upstairs, leaving the younger with Oban and his old DVD collection. Through the creaky boards and enhanced acoustics of the old house, he heard him speaking in muffled tones to whom he assumed was Nooriya, on the phone.

The next morning, Aahan rose early, thanks to a hangover, an unfamiliar pillow and the crisp mountain air. He felt simultaneously refreshed and depleted, and momentarily annoyed that his father didn't possess a coffee machine, not even a cafetière, that he would have to make do with instant coffee.

He entered the sunroom for breakfast to see Nooriya seated at the table with Asif. He wondered where she could have gone, to have returned so quickly. Travelling around the hills at night was next to impossible. Had she been there the whole time, in his father's bedroom upstairs? He didn't acknowledge her and joined his father at the table. He looked at her from the corner of his eye, and she caught him. He looked away, and tried to pretend that she wasn't there after that. His father cleared his throat and watched him wolf down eggs, bacon, toast and orange juice. As soon as he had finished, he said, 'I have decided to stay here, Aahan. I have done what I can to give you a start in life. I've given you a running business, the family house, an education, and I'm afraid I have nothing more to give. I cannot do anything further for you, you must sort this mess out for yourself.' He looked at Nooriya, and she nodded imperceptibly, encouragingly.

Aahan looked at him disbelievingly, unable to remove his gaze. The older man's hand trembled as he put down his fork, refusing to meet his son's eye. Nooriya continued to drink tea from a floral tea pot. She put her cup down and rose from her seat.

'It is time for us to go for our walk, Janu,' she said, making no more effort to engage with Aahan than he had done with her. Aahan got up and went to his room, picked up his overnight bag, and left for Delhi. Asif wasn't at the gate to bid him farewell.

One day, soon after, while tending to his beloved roses, Asif had a stroke. Nooriya was upstairs, blow-drying her chin-length hair, as she always did, though there was no one in Shimla to see. She saw him crumple from the window, rose cutter in hand, and ran down, half her damp hair sectioned in clips and the other half coiffed. They drove straight to Chandigarh and admitted him at a hospital there.

Nooriya told no one. Aahan wasn't in touch with his father.

Nooriya kept a constant vigil on him, moving into the hospital with her suitcase and vanity kit, painstakingly applying makeup, doing her hair, and wearing sarees every day. He deteriorated steadily, and the bills mounted. Nooriya didn't have access to Asif's funds. She called Laxman and informed him that he had a stroke, not the money part of course, that wasn't his place.

Laxman entered Aahan's cabin without knocking, tears in his eyes, and apprised him of the developments. Aahan phoned Divya.

'Papa is dying, Divya. It's time,' he said.

Aahan graciously stepped in, and arrived at the hospital, facing Nooriya for the second time in the year. He was polite and called her Aunty.

'Aunty, don't worry at all. Why not go up to Shimla, take a short break? I am here now, plus, there are nurses to take care of Papa,' he said.

Nooriya was exhausted. Not a young woman herself, she longed for a night of sleep in her own bed. The hospital sofa-cum-bed had killed her back. The hospital had no shower, and she had been bathing with a half-bucket of hot water and a mug. Her silver roots were clearly visible on her hairline, she would have liked to attend to that, Asif shouldn't see her like that when he awoke.

'I desperately need a hot shower, some proper rest, and then I will be back to look after him, just a couple of days,' she said to Aahan, and, leaving Asif in his son's care, began the winding journey up to the mountains.

While Nooriya was with Aahan, unbeknownst to her, Divya paid a visit to the Shimla house. She alighted from her car and took a deep breath of the pine-scented air, and noticed that her father's beloved roses were dying. No one had deadheaded them.

The staff there had been around since she was a child. She remembered the old couple fondly, as they did her.

'*Papa ko Dilli le ke ja rahen hain, Kaka. Wahan ilaj accha hain*,' she told the caretaker of the property. '*Apni dekhbhaal ke liye rakh lo, pata nahin ab kab aayenge*,' she continued, rummaging in her oversized handbag, and handing a lakh of rupees each in cash in identical white envelopes with Sikand

Automotives embossed on them in green to the three retainers in the house. Divya began to pack anything that could have belonged to a woman in her father's bedroom into large black garbage bags that she had brought with her. No one tried to stop her, this was the sahib-log's matter, and it was best not to get involved. She packed hastily, and callously, not bothering to click shut the cap of Nooriya's conditioner bottle, which she threw into a bag with her silk saris, tossing a half-eaten box of chocolates into another bag for good measure. She collected the multiple photos of the Babaji-type that Nooriya followed, which were littered through the house, and threw them in a separate carton. She contemplated burning her possessions, but then decided against it, she didn't actually know how to carry that out, and it might delay her. She did not want to run into Nooriya. Security guards from an expensive security agency in Chandigarh had been employed, beefy looking bouncers. They carried the bags down the stairs, to the outhouse, and locked the main house with the new locks that she had brought with her. Divya kept the keys in her bag. Nooriya and her son were not to be allowed in, and her possessions were to be handed over to her, she briefed the security guards who took control of the outhouse.

She bid the caretaker farewell, gently chiding him for not tending to her father's roses, and proceeded to the hospital in Chandigarh, invigorated by the cause, finally showing that woman her place. She would find out soon enough. Nooriya's and Divya's cars passed each other in the crowded Shimla bazaar, though each was too engrossed in their own thoughts to notice the other.

Aahan and Divya, with consent letters from their mother and other sisters, as the next of kin, discharged their father on their own responsibility, and took him back to Sikand House, where the guest room, which he had claimed as his own all those years ago, had been prepared for him, with a hospital-style bed and round-the-clock nursing care. Their father would die in Sikand House, with his rightful wife by his side.

Unable to access the house in Shimla, Nooriya had tried Aahan's number, the one that he had given her a missed call from, when she had left the hospital a few hours ago, but it had automatically disconnected. He must have blocked her. She tried him from the driver's phone, but he hung up when he learnt it was her, and didn't answer again. Unsure of what to do, she returned to the hospital in Chandigarh to find the Sikand family gone. In a daze, she had proceeded to Delhi; she still had access to her flat there. She needed to find Asif, and was ready to camp outside Sikand House until they let her meet him. She rang Aman, but he wasn't in Mumbai, he had gone to Ibiza with a fashion-designer friend. She told him the news, and summoned him back. He would see what he could do, he didn't have a ticket, and had travelled with his friend and a bunch of people on a chartered aircraft.

Asif deteriorated further, he hadn't taken the journey well. The end was near.

Nobody from his first family told Nooriya when Asif had a massive heart attack, that he was gone, that mourners could come to Sikand House between 11 a.m. and 2 p.m. to pay their last respects. After decades of companionship, love, togetherness, and a beautiful son, she learnt of this news through an obituary printed in the *Hindustan Times* the next day, with his birth name, and with his first family mourning him, obliterating any trace of Nooriya or Aman from his life.

She had to see him, she had to go to Sikand House. She decided to call upon Laxman Kumar for help. She tried his number from the landline, apprehensive that he wouldn't answer. He picked up the unknown number, so many arrangements were to be made. There was commotion on his end. When he learnt that it was Nooriya on the phone, he said, '*Madam, kuch sunaiye nahin de raha, bas abhi wapas phone karta hoon*.' He didn't, and wouldn't pick up any of her calls after that.

She drove past Sikand House and saw another set of burly, heavy-set bouncers at the gate. She slowed down, but they had recognized her, and she instead asked them directions to a nearby address and drove away. Aimlessly driving about, she passed a narrow, congested market and looked mindlessly into the shops on the side of the road. A halal meat shop, stationery mart, several tailors, a cyber cafe, and a garment shop with colourful burqa-clad mannequins in different postures, and had one clad in bubblegum-pink that was pointing her index finger cheerfully into the middle distance, quite like a B.R. Ambedkar statue, she thought. She suddenly swerved right into a gully, scratching the edge of her car against the kerb, parked and got out. She walked into the garment store, and later emerged in a black burqa, just her eyes visible, hailed an auto-rickshaw, and gave the driver the address of Sikand House.

Arriving at the gates once again, she saw a stream of people enter the premises, several of whom she recognized. Nooriya told the auto-wallah to wait, to keep the meter running. They would have to come out sometime. A while later, a hearse slowly drove out from inside the premises, the driveway just wide enough to let it through safely. Rajesh and Laxman were helping the driver navigate out of the tight space, and then they jumped in, Rajesh in the front with the driver, and Laxman at the back. Aahan must be inside with his father, she speculated, and thought of Aman, who still hadn't returned. The disinterested auto driver was asked to follow the hearse. At the crematorium, she followed the procession, unbeknownst to the first family.

The air around the crematorium was grey with the Delhi winter haze and smoke from the burning pyres. When she approached Asif's body, fell at his feet and kissed them, everyone knew who she was. Her burqa protected her from the world, and no one, not Divya nor Aahan, could pluck up the courage to approach her. Saying her goodbyes, she vowed to get herself and Aman their due.

Aahan tolerated this, hoping that it would be the end of it. The priest finished reciting the prayers, and the body was slowly moved from the initial holding area to a large, covered cremation ground, open at the sides where three other pyres were burning simultaneously. The crowd chanted '*Ram nam satya hai*' in listless, morose unison. Aahan lit his father's pyre. His mother, who had inexplicably insisted on wearing her wedding saree, a blood-red banarsi with pure gold paisley woven into it, was surrounded by his wife and sisters in pristine white designer chikan, and fawn shahtoosh shawls – they had been expecting this day. The first Mrs Sikand was expressionless behind her large sunglasses.

Aahan stood uncomfortably close to the fire. His eyes burnt from the smoke, and the heat emanating from his father's burning body made his face uncomfortably hot. A few sparks occasionally singed his shawl. The mourners, who had come to show solidarity, were getting impatient, having put on their funerary expressions and low voices for long enough, waiting to show Aahan that they were there. Some people began gossiping in muted tones, an occasional smile appearing and quickly disappearing from their faces. An acquaintance could wait no longer, he had a flight to catch. He pushed through the crowd and approached Aahan, just a couple of feet away from where the pyre burnt. Aahan had registered and acknowledged his presence, and thanked him for coming. He was now free to go.

This initiative emboldened others. One by one, mourners started approaching the pyre, attempting to stay in a single line, while uncomfortably manoeuvring the narrow passage between where Aahan was standing, and his father's now blazing pyre. Rajesh took it upon himself to manage the flow of people, ensuring that one person returned before the next went. When a burkha-clad woman approached, Rajesh let her pass.

Nooriya approached Aahan, who had been mechanically accepting the mourners' condolences. He saw a figure in black, who raised her veil as she approached him. As his eyes met hers, a lifetime of absences and excuses and petty humiliations flashed by. Quite unplanned, he shoved her hard, and she fell onto the edge of the pyre.

Nooriya screamed in pain and surprise. Her synthetic burkha burst into a ball of flames. The crowd gasped. Rajesh lunged towards the fire, pulling Aahan's shawl along the way, and rolled Nooriya onto the cool ashes of the next pyre, awaiting collection by family members. He covered her tightly with the shawl. They rolled around in the ashes, and the fire was extinguished.

Maha-Maharajji ki kripa, she was alive.

'Aahan, what have you done?' screeched a stunned Parul.

The moments between Nooriya tripping onto the fire and Rajesh saving her were all black for Aahan. He looked at Parul blankly.

Parul's uncle, her Mausaji, stepped in to help. Nooriya was bundled into the same hearse that had brought Asif's body to the crematorium, and sent to his clinic. Mausaji's clinic staff was mobilized. They had their ways, and didn't report the case to the police.

Maha-Maharajji ki kripa, her burns were mostly second-degree. The pain was excruciating, and even contact with air seemed to hurt. She was all alone with no one there to help her. No one thought to reach Aman. Nooriya's phone couldn't be located, everyone forgot about it, and then him.

In the hazy first few days, when Mausaji had guards at the doors, it was Sana who was allowed to enter. She kept a vigil over her, present, but self-sufficient, like a cat. Mausaji didn't want to mess with a political type, and there was no reason for her to be alone, he reasoned with Aahan, she was the aggrieved party here. Nooriya was heavily sedated, and barely registered her presence. Sana continued to work on her laptop, the ashram was to host a large pravachan for Indian-Americans, in Edison, New Jersey, soon, and she had been named the in-charge by the AMC – a real honour. They would fly her to America too, her first visit back after her overnight wedding.

Nooriya would sometimes babble incoherently but Sana couldn't decipher most of it – it was in Hindi, not her strong point at the best of times, but impossible to follow with an incoherent person. 'Aman' and 'Jaanu' was all that was comprehensible in her initial soundtrack. Sana just pretended it wasn't happening, and continued with her work.

Nooriya began to recover. She registered Sana and smiled feebly. 'Aman, 9820422765,' she said repeatedly, until Sana tuned in, wrote the number on her palm and WhatsApped a picture of it to Rajesh.

Rajesh passed it on to Chotu, and dictated a text to be sent, anonymously: 'Mother serious. Come immediately. Blessings Nursing Home, L-32, GK I, New Delhi.'

On the mend, with her son by her side, Nooriya asked Sana to connect her to the ashram legal team. An obituary was printed in the newspaper, Nooriya Sikand and Aman Sikand mourning a loving husband and father, with a picture of him from the Shimla garden in springtime.

She summoned Aahan to her bedside. Mausaji, who had been keeping tabs on the situation, firmly suggested that he comply, he had done his bit, and wanted her out of his nursing home without any further trouble.

'Aahan, I have always tried to stay out of your family's way, and that's all I wanted in return, but you and that Divya have always had it in for me, the results of which are there for all to see,' she said. 'Is it my fault that your father didn't want your mother anymore? Why isn't it his fault? Or hers, for not being able to keep her man interested? Or what if it is nobody's fault? Maybe your father loved me, and not her, or maybe he loved us all, or maybe he felt he had to love your family more because they came first?' Anger flashed on Aahan's face. This was going nowhere. He clenched his fist, and got up to leave.

'Anyhow, I tried to ignore it because of my love for your father,' continued Nooriya. 'He was married off to your mother first, that was circumstantial, but we actively made the choice to be together, difficult as it was. If all of you had cared for how he felt the way he cared about your feelings, his life would have been different, more peaceful, happier. He is gone now, and I don't owe any of you any courtesy. I'll get to the point, I want a share of Sikand House for Aman. It's his right too, he is a Sikand too, whether you lot like it or not. It's your father that made you a Sikand, not your mother, and it's just the same for Aman. I'm not an unreasonable person, but if you don't comply, I will file a case under the Sati Act against you. I've explored the options, I'm not just talking crazy. It happened. You have pushed me onto my husband's pyre. The punishment is life imprisonment. There are enough witnesses, you know.'

The burns on the left side of her face stung. 'If you do as I say, this ends here, I tripped and fell onto the pyre.'

Aahan said nothing, and stared at her. Most of her body was under the hospital sheet. Her arms had silicone patches all over them, and he could tell that they had no muscle tone, and sagged with age.

'You did nothing? You did nothing? You took my father and turned him into an Asif for fuck's sake. Nooriya, or whatever it is that you call yourself, you are mistaken if you think you have seen the worst that I can be,' he declared though clenched teeth. Mausaji had been clear that there was to be no drama at the clinic, there were other patients to consider. 'And you think I'm going to hand over my family's house to you, just like that? And to that chhakka son of yours? Dream on, woman.' He spat viciously on the floor, and left the room.

Later that evening, Rajesh visited him at the house, without Laxman. The guard let him in instantly, without checking if he was expected. Rajesh was something of a legend for all the domestic staff who worked at Sikand House.

He walked past the garden, on the tree bark path, and a young maali stopped him for a selfie. He complied, and appreciated that all you could see from any spot at Sikand House was trees and foliage, no matter where on the plot you stood, it was surrounded by parks on each side.

In the living room, he hesitated momentarily, and then sat down on an intricately carved chair, original furniture from the Rai Bahadur's ancestral home in Pakistan. It was surprisingly solid and heavy under his frame, way heavier than it had looked all those years ago. He waited briefly, and Aahan joined him. The two men shook hands and then hugged awkwardly. Rajesh wondered again whether to sit down, and then did.

No further pleasantries were exchanged. '*Bhaiya, aap Nooriya madam se settle kar lo, problem ho jayegi*,' he advised. '*Pehle se cases hain, factory ke, Papa ne bataya*.' Aahan registered Laxman's impertinence. He had spoken to Mausaji's contact, the senior counsel helping him with his other cases, who had informed him that his options were minimal. He had also made it abundantly clear that criminal law was not his specialty, he would have to refer him on to someone else, another colleague who would charge his full fees, as he did not appear in the lower courts, no matter what.

'Rajesh, I'll never let her enter this house,' Aahan said, and then repeated himself in Hindi, '*Mein use kabhi is ghar me ghusne nahin doonga*.'

'*Haan, to mat karo*. But you will have to pay her, settle the matter, or there will be big problems,' said Rajesh.

'Don't take tension, Bhaiya, I'll get the deal done at a reasonable figure, yeh meri guarantee hai,' he assured.

Maha-Maharajji had taken samadhi, but the ashram continued to flourish. The Maharaj had been a bachelor, but the children of his siblings had tried to move in to control the land and trust, no matter that they had been banned from entering the premises in his lifetime, but they were swiftly dealt with. The trustees, who were the members of the AMC, controlled all the ashram's land and assets.

Though she was a lifetime member and trustee, Nooriya had been out of the daily politics of the trust for a while now. The move to Shimla, Asif's illness and demise, with the drama surrounding it, and then her own recovery, had taken its toll, and other people had asserted themselves, usurped the space that she had carved out for herself. Nooriya didn't even know when the meetings took place these days, and what had become of her old office at the trust. She still had her smart card, and the asharam was the first place she went to visit, on her way home, when she was discharged from the clinic. Maha-Maharajji's aura was still the strongest there, it was his aura was had saved her. She arrived at the ashram, and went straight towards her old office, and entered to find Sana behind her old desk, peering at a laptop from behind thick-rimmed spectacles, a jhola hanging behind the chair.

It wasn't lost on Nooriya that Sana, the daughter-in-law of her husband's former servant, was in her chair now. Sana was on the phone, and gestured to her to sit down. Nooriya instead wandered over to the small white window, and saw a box with her things placed on the ledge. She pretended not to notice, and looked down at a bright playground where a few toddlers were playing, accompanied by a young teacher and a couple of ayahs in matching green salwar kameezes with white, starched dupattas in a crisp V ushering them about.

Sana finished her call. 'Perhaps I should have knocked?' said Nooriya, as Sana walked over and hugged her. She winced at the touch under her clothes, her skin hadn't healed completely yet, and recoiled.

'I am so sorry, I didn't mean to hurt you!' said Sana, taking a step back.

'Sit, sit, please, what will you have to drink? So good to see you up and about,' she said, still flustered by causing the older woman pain, and ushered her towards her desk. 'I can't thank you enough, Sana, for looking after me,' began Nooriya.

Sana cut her short. 'I didn't look after you, Maha-Maharajji did. We are a family here, and will always be there for our elders.' She smiled.

'Sana, I would like to come back, to be active again,' said Nooriya, just as Sana had turned around to pick up the box that she knew to contain her things.

Sana didn't respond to her last statement. Instead, she handed the cardboard box to Nooriya, and wished her a quick recovery. An alarm rang on Sana's phone. 'It's time for me to pick my older one up from school, but it was great to see you, Nooriya,' she said.

She had neither beauty nor position nor money to offer now. When she looked at herself in the mirror, Nooriya didn't recognize the woman looking back, with scarred, sagging, greying skin, and a shock of white roots. But she would fight, fight until the end, for Aman, even if he wasn't interested, for Asif, and for the family that they once were. 'Beta, was Rajesh able to speak to him yet?' she asked Sana as they both walked towards the door.

THIRTEEN

RAJESH HAD BEEN able to turn the run in with the PP about the Guneeta problem to his advantage. He discharged his ministerial duties efficiently. His lifelong exposure to sahib-log meant that he knew how to deal with them better than most ruffians in the party. He made money, of course, no one expected him not too, but not too much, within reason, not enough to raise eyebrows. His approach was, at least at this point, to secure his family, rather than to make as much money as he could, a folly that had torpedoed many a politician before his career could begin. Their wives suddenly went from Alto to Mercedes, from shopping in Lajpat Nagar to shopping at Emporio, trailed by some sweaty businessman or the other, who would be paying in cash. There was the legend of one such politician from Jharkhand, who had compelled a mining baron to buy twenty-seven identical Cartier watches for his daughter's in-laws as a part of her dowry.

Naturally, this sort of behaviour tended to attract undue attention, jealousies, and led to their eventual downfall. He was surprised that his colleagues couldn't see this. Luckily for him, these things didn't interest either Sana or his parents. Sana was too much of a drifter to ever miss security – she couldn't miss what she had never had, after all. She was content in the world she had created for herself, with having a family for the first time, and her work at the ashram. As for Laxman and Babita, they had come such a long way that even dreaming of anything more was a travesty.

Fresh elections were just a couple of years away, though, and anything could happen, as always. Rajesh knew that the first thing he would have to acquire was a house, well a flat really, a house was too much, too conspicuous, and would raise too many eyebrows. It was beyond his current reach anyway, in the neighbourhoods that he wanted. He had a reasonable assessment of his own street value. He could have put his children in an international school, with the expats, they were foreign citizens after all. But he decided to put them into the most highly regarded local schools, where admission was much more fiercely competitive, giving the best of people sleepless nights. He wanted them to network with the children of the most prominent Indian families, not waste their time with expats who were bound to leave soon anyway. With his new-found position, he was able to place his children in the finest school in the city, rubbing shoulders with sahib-log's children. Another step towards acceptance. He knew what an address meant to these people, and decided that he would rather get a smaller flat in a tony colony rather than a larger one in a less acceptable colony. That, along with Sana's Americanness, was sure to complete their gentrification. He allowed himself a rare daydream, where he came home from work, and just like in those American TV shows Sana was always watching, she was baking brownies in the kitchen and the children were playing contentedly as he took her, smelling like chocolate, to their bedroom where they slept together, and she loved it.

He had helped a couple of builders with their labour problems, and it was time to pull in a favour. He knew that most of their projects, which were in the older colonies – where he would like to live – were with families with distressed finances looking to upgrade their crumbling houses, separate joint families to satisfy warring sisters-in-law, or to settle debts or inconvenient sisters who insisted on a share in the family's wealth. They usually gave them a flat or two, in exchange for rebuilding the house. The builders had their own financial model, and sold the houses at a huge profit with minimal investment. They would have to oblige him with one of these, all for his past and continued goodwill.

He began to make enquiries, and there were a number of possibilities to consider, some better and some worse. He went, alone, without Sana or his parents, to check out the options. It would be more discreet, and he didn't believe in decision by consensus – he was the captain of the ship now, and everyone would have to make the best of whatever he decided and provided.

He saw huge apartments facing large highways, and smaller ones facing quiet parks. The builder had put a price on what he was worth, and was shown places accordingly.

At one such meeting, he took the builder into confidence about the problems at Sikand House. With the right offer, it would be for sale. It was a prime property, a landmark in the neighbourhood, uniquely positioned with parks on either side.

'*Iss property mein dispute hone wala hai, abhi acche price mein utha lo*,' he advised the builder. 'I will do the talking, *baat mein karaoonga, aur jab banega tab isme ek flat mera. Lekin yeh baat abhi kisi ko nahin batana, keep it quiet, nahin to deal nahin ho payegi*,' he warned. It was better than what the builder would give him otherwise, but his brokering the deal would up his stake.

This would be it. Three bedrooms, one for him and Sana, one for his parents, and one for his children. More than enough for his needs.

He called Aahan and made the proposal, this is how the money would be found to give Nooriya. He came with the builder and his munshi to Sikand House once again.

'*Sikand sahib, kya plot hain!*' began the builder. '*Aap socho hum apna ghar samajh ke banayenge*, we will build it like for our own family, Sir ji. *Koi kami hi nahin hogi*, all first-class bana ke denge, all facilities, luxuries hi kaho, terrace mein jacuzzi, pool, imported modular kitchen, aap khush-khush rahoge.'

Aahan looked at the sweaty, safari-suited, Rolexed man with a shock of dyed black hair with disdain. He poured himself a whiskey and didn't offer any to the others. They all sat down.

'*Woh sab to theek hai, lekin pehle len-den ki baat to final kar lo.* Let's talk figures,' replied Rajesh. '*Ek number aur do number ka break-up bhi important hai,*' he continued. The other flats in the building were to be sold too, Rajesh gleaned through the meeting, and after this deal went through, he and Aahan would have an equal share in the erstwhile Sikand House, square foot for square foot.

The builder took possession of the property, accompanied by Rajesh. It was still undisturbed by the destruction to come, before it would presumably rise like a modern-day steel-and-glass phoenix.

Aahan, he learnt, had been told that Rajesh would be getting a flat alongside him.

Rajesh walked around the premises, a conqueror who had arrived at an abandoned city and seized it without shedding a drop of blood. He saw the old servant quarters, and the garage, where they used to congregate for a bidi and gossip. He started poking around the house, looking into the bedrooms, the upstairs living room where he had first watched television. He entered Aahan's old bedroom and looked out of the window, at the gardens below, and the semal tree from which they had collected cotton snow as children. He took out a shiny black pen, gilded in gold, from his front pocket, and wrote 'Rajesh Kumar' on the wall.

He bid farewell to the builder, and stopped on the way home at a Bengali sweet shop to buy mithai before telling his family. He got chamchams, Sana's favourite.

ACKNOWLEDGEMENTS

Akhil Sibal, my oxygen and enabler-in-chief.

Meru Gokhale, Neerja Pant and Namita Gokhale, for everything, always.

Promilaa and Kapil Sibal, for their love and friendship.

The Bhandares, the Misras and the Pants, you are my world.

Mita Kapur, who saw this through.

Team HarperCollins, Udayan Mitra and Prerna Gill, for believing in my work. Bonita Vaz-Shimray and Trinankur Banerjee for bringing the cover alive.

Ravi Singh, Patrick French and Faiza Sultan Khan, your encouragement came when I needed it the most.